TOUCH

OF

AMBER

JAYNE RYLON

eBook ISBN: 978-1-941785-40-9
Print ISBN: 978-1-941785-72-0

Ebook Cover Art By Angela Waters
Photography By Sophia Renee
Print Book Cover Art By Jayne Rylon
Interior Print Book Design By Jayne Rylon

Sign Up For The Naughty News!
Contests, sneak peeks, appearance info, and more.
www.jaynerylon.com/newsletter

Shop
Autographed books, reading-themed apparel,
notebooks, totes, and more.
www.jaynerylon.com/shop

Contact Jayne
Email: contact@jaynerylon.com
Website: www.jaynerylon.com
Facebook: Facebook.com/JayneRylon
Twitter: @JayneRylon

OTHER BOOKS BY JAYNE RYLON

DIVEMASTERS
Going Down
Going Deep
Going Hard

MEN IN BLUE
Night is Darkest
Razor's Edge
Mistress's Master
Spread Your Wings
Wounded Hearts
Bound For You

POWERTOOLS
Kate's Crew
Morgan's Surprise
Kayla's Gift
Devon's Pair
Nailed to the Wall
Hammer it Home

HOTRODS
King Cobra
Mustang Sally
Super Nova
Rebel on the Run
Swinger Style
Barracuda's Heart
Touch of Amber
Long Time Coming

COMPASS BROTHERS
Northern Exposure
Southern Comfort
Eastern Ambitions
Western Ties

COMPASS GIRLS
Winter's Thaw
Hope Springs
Summer Fling
Falling Softly

PLAY DOCTOR
Dream Machine
Healing Touch

STANDALONES
4-Ever Theirs
Nice & Naughty
Where There's Smoke
Report For Booty

RACING FOR LOVE
Driven
Shifting Gears

RED LIGHT
Through My Window
Star
Can't Buy Love
Free For All

PARANORMALS
Picture Perfect
Reborn

PICK YOUR PLEASURES
Pick Your Pleasure
Pick Your Pleasure 2

DEDICATION

For people who aren't afraid to go against the flow and take some calculated risks.

CHAPTER ONE

Amber Brown tapped a stylus against her tablet. She neatly checked the empty boxes remaining beside the items on her inventory sheet as she confirmed the corresponding crate had been stowed beneath the bus about to depart. Each box had been carefully packed and logged to ensure the essentials made it to their destination.

"I think this is the last of them. Number 25-C of the green labels," Kaige—her future brother-in-law—told her as he reached over her shoulder and poked the designated entry on her list. If his lip curled in a bit of a grin behind the fall of his blond dreadlocks, she ignored his mockery of her complex system.

It was his damn fault she was short-staffed, since he'd stolen her sister away from Brown & Brown. On top of that, Amber's brand-spanking-new replacement partner was one of the four brides boarding the Wedding Partymobile the Hot Rods mechanics had retrofitted for this special trip.

She never would have guessed the sleek monstrosity in front of her had started its life as a bright yellow school bus. Then again, this gang had a way of transforming most things— and people—they touched.

"Thanks." She smiled despite her gritted teeth until he turned away to assist her pregnant sister up the stairs. As soon as his attention had winged back to his fiancée, she scrubbed the offending fingerprint he'd left on the shiny surface of her tablet with the oyster-hued silk of her long-sleeved blouse. Anal? Yup. But she liked things precisely as they should be. Habitual organization contributed to her success.

How else could a single event planner survive the coordination of a quadruple unconventional destination wedding without going absolutely bonkers? Then again, she hadn't pulled it off just yet.

It was nearly impossible to concentrate with the chaos that constantly swirled around her when she entered the Hot Rods' domain. Eight sexy mechanics, their feisty mates, a kid brother and even a puppy—not to mention their dad, who kept causing Amber's own mother to swoon with a series of steamy stares. Together, they made for one big, noisy, rowdy—and, admittedly, fun—group.

It was her job to wrangle them.

She deserved a raise.

"Quinn, grab Buster McHightops's leash. You're in charge of him until we get to Bare Natural, okay?" She smiled at the teenager, who wouldn't mind dog-sitting one bit. In fact, he seemed to stand a bit taller knowing she trusted him to take responsibility for the shop's mascot.

"Sure, Amber." He offered her a sheepish smile as he and the puppy trundled toward the bus stairs, which had been painted in a Hot Rods' version of polka dots—skulls and fireballs—courtesy of Mustang Sally. He hadn't said much about their trip, but he'd been the first one packed and ready to leave for their mini-vacation, even though the naturist resort was closed, reserved exclusively for their festivities.

The allure of naked breasts had nothing on fishing, romping through the woods and hanging out with his big brother. Especially for a kid who'd never experienced any of those fundamental delights.

"Hang on. Come here a second, please." Amber curled her fingers until he whipped around.

"Yeah?"

She wrapped him in a one-armed hug and squeezed before he pulled back, startled.

3

"What was that for?" He seemed unsure of how to react as his cheeks reddened.

"Because I like you." She also knew what it was like to shoulder worry beyond your years as a child. At least she'd had Nola for company. Going it alone...he must have shared every ounce of Roman's tough genes to have survived. "Now get your ass on that bus or we're going to be late."

"Come on, Buster." Quinn laughed as he raced the dog out of sight.

One of the mirrored bus windows dropped open and Kaelyn's beautiful blue eyes appeared in the gap. "Are you sure you don't need me to help?"

"Yep. Just enjoy the ride. You only get married once." Amber frowned. "Well, I hope. I mean, don't expect me to do this over again if you don't stick it out with Bryce. Perfection isn't easy to arrange."

"And we know you don't settle for anything less." The groom winked at her from behind his fiancée, though they both understood his barb wasn't too far from the truth. Nearly obsessive about control, Amber made the ideal project coordinator. As for her personal life, well, that sucked. Either the same tactics weren't going to cut it on that front or she simply hadn't taken a day off in forever to apply what she'd learned in her professional capacity. She hoped it was that.

Hanging around these crazy couples was starting to make her doubt everything she'd held as fact. They seemed more secure, not less, since falling in love. That made her dream...

Or at least, maybe it would if she ever had time to sleep again.

After these weddings were over, she promised herself. She could survive three more days, right?

Amber closed the hatches, locked them, then took one final look around. She drew a deep breath, straightened her suit's skirt then braced herself before boarding the Partymobile.

Eli London, the garage's owner and unofficial leader of the Hot Rods gang, sat behind the wheel, checking the dials and gauges while his GPS calculated their route.

"All right, Cobra." She smiled at him. "Let me do a roll call and we'll be set to pull out."

"That's what *he* said," Quinn muttered loud enough for his brother, who sat directly behind him, to hear. Roman snorted until Carver glared at him and he tried to snuff the appreciation of his underage sibling's inappropriateness. The two grooms of couple

5

number four were too damn handsome to scold.

That didn't stop Amber's mom, though.

From where she shared a black leather seat with Tom, Eli's dad, at the head of the bus, across the aisle from Quinn and Buster, she whipped around fast enough that Amber wished she could warn the kid of the impending slap down.

"Quinn London!" She shook her finger for added effect, though using his new family's name helped mitigate her outrage. "Is that any way to talk? You've been listening to those Powertools guys too much lately. I'm going to have to set them straight when we get there."

The teenager groaned and covered his face as if apologizing in advance to their mutual friends. "Sorry, Ms. Brown."

"That's better," she huffed.

Tom was quick to distract her from her ire, coming to Quinn's rescue with a grin and a wink over Willie's head.

Behind the more traditional seating up front, the gang had worked their magic, turning the back of the bus into some sort of lounge. It looked entirely too decadent for Amber, considering her sister was one of the women curled up between the hunks who occupied far more than their fair share of the couches.

Tangled together, their bodies became indistinguishable in the dusky interior. Black leather, plush midnight carpet and a matching high ceiling made the space intimate and private as could be. On purpose, she was sure.

"Listen up!" Amber's shout cut through the rumble of their chatter. "I'm making sure nobody's left behind. Sally!"

No one answered, though she could clearly see the woman perched on Alanso's lap, making out with her husband—well, one of them, since Eli was driving. Her fingers were splayed on the bald man's head, keeping him close even when he tried to acknowledge Amber's shout.

Thank God she'd have a seat to herself to focus on work so she could ignore the barrage of pheromones that seemed to hover around this gang like a cloud, poisoning Amber's ambition with dangerous wishes for a distraction of that caliber.

Finally Holden kicked Alanso's scuffed motorcycle boot with a steel-toe of his own. "Come on, dude. There will be plenty of time for that once we're on the road. It's not like you're gonna be able to take care of business anyway. Try not to torture yourself. Sooner we leave, sooner we get there."

If she could see better in the dim lighting, Amber would have sworn she caught a feral gleam in the eyes of the men from where she stood. She shivered at the raw power of their desire, even though it wasn't aimed at her.

"Sally," Amber said again as she ticked off the female mechanic from her list.

"Use her *real* name and I bet she'll answer," Bryce teased.

"Mustang!" Amber humored them.

"Yep. I'm here." The woman stopped feasting on Al long enough to flash a thumbs-up.

Amber chuckled along with the rest of the gang.

She rolled her eyes and called next to Alanso, though she could plainly see him. Methodical, she refused to skip a step even if it was obvious.

"Kaige...er...Nova?" she amended.

"Reporting for duty, ma'am!" He offered her a salute that had Nola bursting into a fit of giggles.

"I'm here too, sis." She saved Amber a step.

"Bryce?" Amber groaned. "I mean, Rebel."

"I'm onboard. And so is Kae. Not getting out of my sight until she's officially mine." He beamed at his lovely bride-to-be before they also deteriorated into a make-out session.

"Swinger?"

Holden grinned and called back, "Yep. I'm in the house. Well, the sweet Partymobile, anyway."

"You've got me too, Amber." His fiancée, Sabra, piped up from where she was wedged into the corner of the couch between two guys. Amber might have assumed she'd broken a limb to contort into that position, except the unusual pose was hardly a stretch for the yoga expert. A skill that must come in handy in their group bedroom gymnastics, Amber figured. She slammed the door on that meandering thought before she could visualize her sister's involvement in the sexual side of their obviously electric relationship.

"Barracuda and Meep," she finished, nodding as she looked over at Roman and Carver. The pair snuggled into their private seat behind Quinn, their hands entwined as they wore huge, matching grins.

"Ready for takeoff," Carver barked.

"Very ready," Roman agreed.

Amber ignored their insinuations and gave Eli the okay to go. "That's all fifteen of us. Plus the dog."

"Poor Fuzzi." Sabra lamented her cat, who would be holding down the Hot Rods' apartment while they were away, watched by a local pet sitter in their absence.

"Are you kidding? That cat's not going to know what to do with all that space to itself. It's going to love every minute of dog-free time it can get." Holden knew exactly how to salve Sabra's guilt.

"You're right about that." She smiled. "Maybe I just need to be distracted for a while until the house is out of sight."

"I can manage that." Holden leaned in and whispered something—undoubtedly naughty—in his lover's ear.

"You kids behave yourselves!" Tom bellowed from the front seat before they'd even gotten out of the parking lot. "Don't make me have my son turn this bus around or you'll be sorry!"

Everyone laughed.

Amber included. Tom was one of the greatest guys she'd ever met. If her mom had to fall for anyone, she was glad it looked like it might be him. Maybe. They'd been dancing around each other for months. Willie deserved a break in the love department.

Don't you too? a small part of her wondered until she muted the rogue thought.

Before sitting down, Amber told everyone what she'd been working on that morning. "I packed a cooler over there full of snacks. I made each of you your favorite sandwiches. There are drinks too, marked with your names—the uncool ones, sorry. It's a five-hour drive, so whenever you get hungry, dig in."

"That was really sweet of you. Thanks, Amber." Carver smiled from his seat across the aisle from her.

"More like efficient. That way we won't have to lose time stopping more than once for a bathroom break when Alanso takes over driving halfway as planned. I have a lot to do when we arrive." She might have sounded brusque, but it was only honest.

"You hear that, boys?" Meep yelled over his shoulder. "If any of you smuggled some beer on board, and I'd be disappointed if you didn't, you'd better pace yourselves. This bus is only making one pit stop."

"Fuck. I told you we should have built a bathroom," Bryce grumbled from the rear.

"Next time." Kaige added, "I think we could do a pretty good business selling these rigs to limo companies. Add it to the business plan, Nola."

"Already beat you to it, babe," she answered.

Those two practically thought with one brain. Amber smiled as she prepared to tune them out so she could finalize the seating chart, confirm the flower deliveries and respond to several dozen other emails from vendors and service providers so that no detail was left unattended.

After that she had to pay some invoices and enter a crap ton of receipts into her accounting software. Plenty to keep her busy for the entire trip.

***

Amber checked her watch a long time later, lifting her head briefly to study the road signs they whizzed past. They were making good time. Getting close. She might pick up a half hour if Alanso kept up this pace.

She stretched, having finally finished her administrative duties. Beside her, Carver and Roman were playing a video game on their tablet. Quinn had his headphones on and was rocking out. Tom and her mom hadn't stopped chatting the entire ride.

Turning around, she spied most of the adults crashed out, taking advantage of the downtime to catch up on their rest. Under other circumstances, she suspected they'd have amused themselves with pleasuring each other. Between that and the crazy hours they'd been putting in at the shop in anticipation of their stint away, they had to be half as exhausted as she was.

Feeling decadent, she neatly rolled her sweater into a soft log, put it against the window, then rested her head on it. Her eyelids immediately drooped as she planned to make the most of the remaining travel time. If she got in a power nap now, she could stay up later tonight, working on the decorations at the new gazebo the Powertools crew had built to her specifications for the ceremony.

Except she swore she had no sooner closed her eyes than a loud bang snapped them wide open once more. The explosive sound was immediately followed by them jerking hard to the right then back to the left as they fishtailed. Her face rapped against the window. Alanso cursed as Eli shouted for his mate.

Tires screeched and rapid-fire Spanish filled the bus as Alanso wrestled the beast to the side of the road. They came to a stop with a lurch. The scent of burning rubber stung the inside of her nose.

"Holy shit! Al!" Eli burst from the rear of the bus to the front before Amber could orient herself. "What happened? Are you okay?"

Meanwhile, Roman was asking her the same. Tenderly, she poked at her cheekbone, then winced. It would probably make a bit of a bump later, but she seemed fine. Everyone else too, thank God.

They began to disembark, each of them hugging the tree line as far from the highway as possible while Eli, Kaige and Bryce surveyed the damage. Her mom fussed unnecessarily over the rising knot on Amber's face until the guys returned to give Tom a report.

"Some asshole in front of us didn't have his load secured," Alanso explained. "I saw the ladder starting to slide, but I couldn't get out of the way entirely. It landed stretched out across the whole lane and there were cars on either side of us. *Mierda*!"

"You did the best you could. No one's hurt. It blew one of the tires, that's all." Eli rubbed the back of Alanso's neck as he spoke. "Pretty great driving there, Al."

Kaige looked angry as he wrapped Nola in his arms and rubbed her belly. Still, he was able to keep his temper in check so that he didn't upset his fiancée or their unborn child any more than they'd already been shaken up by the wreck.

Tom glanced around from person to person, nodding as he made sure they were each all right.

"The bad news is that we had to ditch the spare tire to fit in everyone's crap." Bryce groaned. "How bad is it? Maybe we can make a patch to get us to the next exit."

Amber squinted at the shredded tread. She didn't have to be an expert to know there was no way. "You're mechanics, not MacGyver. What do you need? Write it down and I'll call a cab to go pick it up."

She already had her browser open and her finger hovering over the link for the nearest cab company as she mentally calculated the length of the delay and the impact to her schedule. Sabra loomed over her shoulder with her ever-present video camera. At least this would make for some drama on the *Hot Rods* reality show.

"You're not going alone." Eli shook his head. "In fact, this thing is huge. Heavy and dirty, probably. One of us can handle it. Just because you're planning the wedding doesn't mean you're our slave. Jesus. Let someone else do this."

She didn't pay him much mind.

Before she could tap the link and put in a request to the online dispatcher, a loud rumble startled her. She took a few steps farther away from the road. So did everyone else. Buster McHightops barked like a maniac as a motorcycle rolled onto the shoulder.

The damn thing nearly deafened Amber.

Badass and beefy, the bike *was* undeniably sexy. Deep blue metallic paint glinted in the afternoon sunlight and a painting of a lone wolf was revealed when the rider climbed off.

The man who'd wrangled the machine wasn't bad either. His long legs were encased in denim and his charcoal T-shirt was partially obscured by a black leather motorcycle jacket with more zippers than seemed entirely necessary. The contraption made Amber want to bury her nose in it and breathe deep.

When he flipped up his visor, a piercing gaze bored into her as if he could feel her gawking, mentally undressing him in a way she never would have admitted to. The tattoos she glimpsed disappearing into the wrist of his jacket would decorate the solid muscles she could tell were hiding beneath soft cotton.

"Wow," Nola murmured from beside her.

"Hey!" Kaige growled.

"Sorry." She laughed. "I may be taken, but I'm not blind. Besides, I might as well be invisible. He's staring at my sister."

"Is not." Amber turned to Nola, breaking the connection with the newcomer. She felt the snap of it recoiling in her guts as if it had been a physical link. Something about him fascinated her. Drew her in. Made him seem...familiar?

Roman roared and rushed past her to greet the mystery man, putting his arms around the guy's broad, leather-clad shoulders for a brusque man-hug followed by a solid fist bump. No one could hear their exchange in the rush of traffic passing nearby. Eli waved them over to join the rest of the Hot Rods assembled on the shoulder of the highway.

The way the guy swaggered, calm, sure, and with the tiniest hint of a limp, clued her in.

He was familiar because she'd seen him before. Even at a distance, he'd intrigued her.

"This is Gavyn, Kayla's brother."

Amber heard what Roman was saying. Hell, she even knew who the guy was, having noticed him wandering through the background on videochats with the Powertools before. He was living temporarily-but-not-so-temporarily at Bare Natural while he got himself clean, sober and on his feet.

"I swerved to miss that fucking ladder too. On a motorcycle, well, yeah... It'd have hurt more than in your bus, that's for sure. I started to pull over to call the cops so they can pick it up, and that's when I saw your ride. Figured it could only belong to one group of crazy mechanics I know given that paint job." He held out his hand to Roman for a high five. "It's badass. Good job."

Amber still couldn't do more than gape at Gavyn as her mouth went dry and her knees threatened to buckle. *Get it together. Fix the problem. Don't get distracted. Not now.*

She shook her head, pressing the bump that had formed with two fingers when it throbbed softly. And that's when she realized Eli had been explaining their plan.

"No need to call a cab. I'll take you into town. I'm already here. It's no problem." He held out his hand to Amber. She couldn't bring herself to take it. If she did, she might not be able to let go of those strong, thick fingers encased in driving gloves that left his knuckles bare.

Her hesitation went on long enough to be apparent.

"Go ahead, Amber." Her mother betrayed her, her mouth curled up slightly on one side. "The rest of these big lugs aren't going to make very good riding partners for this nice fellow."

"I'm not dressed for..." She rounded on her mom with wide eyes, hoping she could transmit the *what-the-hell-are-you-doing* glare she intended.

"Nothing prettier than a woman in a skirt on the back of a motorcycle," Alanso practically purred. "You're dressed perfectly for this job, *chica*."

And her own damn sister pushed her over the edge. "Go ahead, sis. I dare you."

Because Amber never had been able to refuse a challenge.

"Fine." She marched over to their savior and steeled herself for the full body contact they were about to make as she straddled his wide machine. "I'm counting on you to drive faster than some damn cab."

Both for the sake of her timeline and her sanity.

"You got it." He took her hand, then lifted it to the gap in his helmet, placing a kiss on her knuckles. His lips were warm and demanding enough to make her wonder what it would be like to have his mouth on hers without more than a dozen of their closest friends and family looking on. "Anything for a lady."

Gavyn assisted her up the grassy incline, then watched without blinking as she hiked her skirt to the very tops of her thighs. Why had she thought a pencil skirt was the right choice for today?

"Nice," she thought she heard him murmur before flipping his visor closed and climbing onboard. He kept the motorcycle steady as she scrambled on behind him, loving the feel of the warm metal and leather between her legs.

"Closer," he instructed as he grasped her hands and placed them on his tight abs. "Hang on tight. We're not going far, but you don't have a helmet and I assume you don't ride much."

More like never.

She'd *never* ridden a motorcycle, or a man, as fine as this one.

Holy shitballs.

Even the new mega-organizing binder she'd had her eye on hadn't excited her as much as Gavyn. *What the hell?* she thought as she hid her smile against his strong shoulder.

Make lemonade.

CHAPTER TWO

Sunlight streamed through the canopy of leaves overhead. Gavyn steered his custom chopper between the golden shafts and took a deep breath. A warm spring day after a long, hard winter plus a smoking hot woman riding his bike with him, hugging him as he took the curves in the road... He couldn't ask for more than that.

Everything seemed new and green and fresh. Maybe because of the quality time he'd spent on introspection lately, or maybe because nature was coming out of hibernation once more.

Either way, he'd take it.

It was great to feel clean for once.

To *be* clean.

At least when surrounded with things this pleasant. It was clear to him now that Kayla, his sister, was the smartest of his siblings. She'd ditched their high-priced lifestyle for something that spoke to her soul. She lived in the mountains at her resort, surrounded by natural beauty, and worked as a masseuse, relieving people's pain. Providing a safe haven for them to express themselves without recrimination.

That was what he should have done instead of listening to the urgings of their father about what the world would require of him—a way to support a wife, a family, carry on their legacy—which had landed him a fancy law degree, a massive paycheck and an even bigger headache to go with it. He'd spent the past ten years listening to divorcing couples spew hatred at each other every minute of his working day, which had expanded to fill nearly all of his waking hours.

No wonder he'd started to drink.

Plenty of people did to cope with the shit life dealt them.

But why the hell hadn't he been able to stop?

The answer to that mystery still eluded him despite several stints in rehab, like the last one, where he'd met Roman Daily. Whether he knew it or not, that guy had changed Gavyn's life. Convinced him it was worth fighting to break his self-destructive cycle.

The woman perched behind him, groping his chest and belly as if her wandering hands were necessary for her safety, seemed like a fitting reward for the fierce battling he'd done—against himself and his urges—lately.

Gavyn was tempted to take the long way to the garage in town. But he didn't. After all, he was trying to be good these days. No lying. No booze. No drugs.

No more one-night stands.

Shit, he might have to rethink that last part.

Not that a woman as classy as his passenger would indulge his base instincts. He sighed as they rolled into the lot of the garage.

Amber practically launched from behind him the moment they came to a stop, as if her ass was spring-loaded. A chuckle rumbled from his chest despite his disappointment at the removal of her heat and clutching hold.

After swinging his leg over the bike and tugging off his helmet, he spun to find her yanking the hopelessly crumpled fabric of her skirt into place somewhere around the middle of her svelte thighs. It didn't do much to obscure the gorgeous lengths of her ultra-long legs.

As discreetly at possible, he adjusted his stiff cock. Not that he minded if she knew how badly he wanted her—more than a drink at the moment, and that was saying something. It was painful, how hard she made him.

He hadn't gotten laid since the bender he'd gone on that had landed him in rehab the last time. That probably didn't help either. But he was honest enough with himself, these days, to admit there was something different about Amber. Something irresistible.

Especially for a man with poor self-control.

"Well…" She cleared her throat. "Thanks for the ride. I've got this from here."

Gavyn laughed. "I'm not going to take off just like that. Come on. Let's go see if they have the size Eli needs. Otherwise, I'll find somewhere else to try."

Amber shrugged, then spun on her sexy black heels. He'd spent enough time around women in suits that he wouldn't have expected to get turned on by one. Usually the brass-balled women he'd crossed paths with were either scheming to steal their husband's fortunes or representing some dickhead who deserved to lose every penny.

This woman had a stick wedged so far up her ass he thought he might be able to see it if she opened her mouth wide enough, but she lacked that killer instinct most of his fellow lawyers—or the cunning, underhanded divorcees he'd had a reputation for representing—had possessed.

The combination of softness over a steel core tempted him to needle her for the sole purpose of seeing what would happen. True, he was short on entertainment these days. No parties, not much to do except think up at his sister's place. So he jogged to catch up to her long strides, then slipped his hand up until it rested against the small of her back.

She shot him a look that promised she'd chop his arm off if he didn't move it quickly.

Gavyn called her bluff.

Too polite to cause a ruckus when they needed assistance, she leveled a glare at him yet kept the magnificent smile on her face as she approached the service station counter, with him right beside her.

"Hey, man." The owner, Marcus, grinned. "Back already? Something wrong with the part?"

"Didn't get to install it yet." Gavyn chuckled. "Found me a stray on the side of the road."

"Gavyn," Amber hissed.

He knew he shouldn't tease her, but he couldn't help himself. It was too damn much fun.

"Somehow I doubt that." Marcus scanned Amber from head to toe. His naked appreciation had Gavyn tightening his hold on her.

"Actually, some douchebag had a ladder unsecured in their truck bed. It flew out and some of my friends hit it. Nothing too major, thankfully. I happened to be coming by and saw them stranded. They blew out a tire on their bus." He shrugged. "I figured you were the best shot at a replacement around here."

"Are these friends the gang that are coming into town for the weddings?" Marcus asked.

"Yup." Gavyn nodded.

"What size?" Marcus asked.

Amber fished in her bag for the neat, precisely folded paper Eli had scrawled the information on. She handed it over to the local mechanic, who hummed and began to pound away on the battered keyboard at his workstation. After about ten thousand keystrokes, he flashed them an okay sign.

"So you have it in stock?" Amber asked.

"Yep," Marcus confirmed.

"How much is it?"

"For the Hot Rods, it's free. Hell, I'll even follow you two out there with the flatbed and deliver it myself." He smiled. "Just make sure you introduce me and say the name of our garage nice and loud on film, huh?"

Gavyn laughed.

"That can be arranged." Amber nodded. She immediately fired off a text on her phone, her manicured nail flying so quickly across the smooth screen that her finger blurred.

Something about her proficiency made him want to get her dirty, messed up. Maybe it would make him feel better about the fact that he couldn't seem to get his own shit together. Ever.

"Just give me a few to haul this out of the storage locker and load up the truck." Marcus gestured to the waiting room. "You can have a seat here if you want. With weather like this, most people prefer the bench over there, though. Whatever works."

Without consulting each other, Amber and Gavyn headed outside. As he held the door for her, he couldn't help but notice the rich vanilla-and-spice scent of her skin. It dared him to lick her. Everything about her turned him on.

"You know these guys?" Amber asked as she perched on the edge of the seat, though it wasn't really a question. "Could have mentioned that."

"Yeah. I've been pestering them with questions, since I'd like to open a shop of my own. One focused on custom bikes." Gavyn tried to play it cool, as if the idea alone hadn't carried him through some rough nights over the past several months.

"That's right." Her eyes lit up at the prospect of a new business. "Kayla asked if I would help you with some strategy for the venture. Between my sister and me, we should be able to come up with something. I just hope I can fit it in with all this wedding stuff. And honestly, because of her experience with the Hot Rods, Nola would probably be better for the job."

"I'd rather have you." He didn't have to lie. Spending time with Amber wouldn't be a hardship. Sexy *and* smart. Now he was really turned on.

"Seriously, she won't mind helping. And she'll have more time than me this week since I've tried to keep everything off her plate so she can relax, enjoy the wedding and make the most of the pre-baby time with Kaige," Amber reasoned.

"Well, if that was your goal, I certainly won't ruin it by hogging her romantic getaway with her groom." He'd been selfish enough these past few years. "What if I help you out and you do the same for me?"

The idea popped into his brain and he'd offered before he even considered it. Once he did, he figured he was some kind of genius. Or more like an idiot savant.

"Hmm?" She peeked up from her phone then and drew her purse tighter to her torso, as if he'd threatened to mug her instead of lightening her load.

"You know, you boss me around during the day. Use me however you like." He wiggled his brows at her. "And when you're finished sooner than you'd otherwise be, we can talk about the shop. Or I could buy you dinner every night and we could discuss it there. Or even later, in bed, if that's your style."

"I don't mix business with pleasure, Gavyn."

"Then forget that other shit and let me kiss you instead." He leaned closer.

"Are you nuts? We just met," she protested, though she seemed to be scrambling for reasons to reject him when he was coming up with an equal number of arguments to the contrary. As if she could sense the stubborn intensity he was about to aim at her, she stood from the bench. So he did too.

"Did you know I'm a lawyer? Well, used to be." He shrugged. "I'm a professional arguer. You're not going to shut me up easily. Unless you put your mouth over mine, anyway. That'll do the trick."

Instead of waiting for her to advance, he did it for her.

For a moment, she didn't seem like she would object.

Amber blinked up at him as he neared, his mouth a hairsbreadth from hers. She sighed, parting her lips and brushing up against him the slightest bit.

Without her tacit approval, he plundered the moist paradise before him. He nibbled on her plump and glossy lower lip before exploring the fullness of her lush mouth well enough to confirm she was delicious. His fingers fisted in her hair, tipping her head back for better access.

It happened fast. From the initial taste of her to him craving a bigger portion. And he wasn't the kind of man used to saying no to himself. Gavyn wrapped his arms around her waist and tugged her flush against his body as he deepened the exchange.

Amber cupped his shoulders with her hands. She didn't use the leverage to push him away, though. Instead, she held him steady when she wrenched her head back and jammed her knee into his balls much quicker than he would have imagined possible.

"Jesus!" He bent in half and swallowed a whole riot of curses as pain assaulted him in waves. He glanced up at her just long enough to make sure she wasn't going to bolt before blackness fuzzed the edges of his vision.

"Oh shit, sorry." Amber put her hands on her cheeks, looking mortified. "It's instinct. I just...I don't let strange guys make out with me in broad daylight like that."

After sucking in a few shaky breaths, he tried to show her he wasn't pissed. Hell, she had been justified, and he admired her strength. "How about after dark?"

"Oh my God!" She pinched the bridge of her nose. "You are absolutely incredible! You know that?"

"Thank you." He grinned, though he knew she hadn't intended her rant as a compliment. Still, he did enjoy verbal sparring. It was about the only thing he'd really excelled at in his life so far.

Muttering under her breath about fool men, Amber marched to his bike, leaving him to scrunch his eyes in pain for a few moments before attempting to straighten up fully. He mumbled, "Son of a motherfucking cocksucker" under his breath while wishing she didn't have quite such good aim.

Which was when the flatbed pulled up next to him, the window open.

"For the sake of your manhood, which has already taken a beating..." Marcus slapped Gavyn on the shoulder. "Let's pretend I didn't see that."

"Good idea." He groaned then walked, slowly and somewhat stooped, over to his bike.

When he got there, he was grateful for the dull ache in his crotch that had him thinking clearly once more because it allowed him to really study Amber, ensuring she was truly pissed off and not upset or afraid. Which was when he noticed the faint bruise shadowing her skin. Her rich complexion had made it difficult to spot before, but now she stood in a wash of light. Instead of molesting her, he should have been making sure she was okay.

"I'm sorry—"

"My fault." He held up his hands as if in surrender. "And I'm not sorry, so you shouldn't be either. It was worth it."

She took a step toward the flatbed as if she'd hitch with Marcus instead. Gavyn caught her elbow. Only long enough to turn her around, not to earn another ball-smashing. This time he was gentle when he reached out, his fingertips brushing her left cheekbone. "Is this from the wreck?"

"Yeah, it's fine." She shrugged.

"I'd like to hear that from an expert. Unless you're a doctor as well as a ninja." He grimaced, knowing she wouldn't much care for his next maneuver. "You're not dizzy or anything, are you? Maybe you shouldn't be riding on the back of my bike."

The thought hurt worse than her kneecap in his nuts, but he wouldn't put her at risk.

"Seriously, it's sore, that's all. A headache. That could just be my luck today, though."

"Okay." He nodded, probably making her think he'd let it go.

But he hadn't.

"Hey, Marcus!" he shouted. "I'm taking Amber to the clinic to get checked out. The Hot Rods are stranded near mile marker 239 on 70, heading east. Can you take care of that?"

"Not a problem." He waved, then left with a roar of his engine that drowned out Amber's protests.

"I don't have time for—"

"Taking care of yourself is top priority. Put yourself first, if only for the hour this will take." He turned serious as he studied her. "Believe me, I've learned that the hard way. And I already told you I'll help you out, be your assistant. Even if you didn't like my terms very much."

This time she didn't argue and surprised the hell out of him by bridging the gap between them and hugging him tight. Sure, it was only for an instant. But it counted.

For once, when she whispered, "Okay. Thank you," he felt like he'd gotten something right.

He'd like to do it more often.

CHAPTER THREE

Amber waved meekly as she entered Dave and Kayla's log cabin past Gavyn, who held the door for her. He'd been surprisingly well behaved since she squashed his boys in a knee jerk reaction. Literally.

She barely had time to say, "Hey," before her mom attacked her, fussing over the blossoming bruise that was doing a fairly good impression of a black eye.

"Seriously, it's nothing major." She hugged her mom quickly, understanding the sheer terror a car accident of any sort infused in the woman considering her husband had been killed in one, scarring her for life.

"You'd say that no matter what," Willie scolded, then turned to Gavyn. "Did you go in the examination room with her?"

"Yes, ma'am," he answered truthfully. No matter how much Amber had tried to get him to stay put, he had followed anyway, convinced—and correct, she might add—that she wouldn't have waited patiently more than two minutes for the doctor before walking right back out again.

"I'll hear it from you then, please." She turned to Gavyn.

Thankfully Amber had anticipated this and coached him on what to say. How to ease her mother's panic without lying outright.

"She's going to be fine. Some bruising. Needs to be a bit careful until it heals, that's all." He carried it off perfectly, failing to mention the hairline fracture in her cheekbone. There wasn't anything to be done to treat it, though Gavyn had promised the doctor she'd take it easier than she'd intended with the weddings happening in less than forty-eight hours.

Which guaranteed they'd be spending most of the next week together. She had no choice but to accept his help on the setup and teardown now. Already she felt sleepy and drained when normally she'd have several more good hours of working before getting fatigued. Damn the timing!

Doubly so because she was afraid Gavyn would be twelve parts distraction to one part assistance.

With him holding her hand at the doctor's office and giving her the broad expanse of his shoulders to lean on for the ride home, he'd offered her comfort and a chance to be a little less...independent than she was used to. Or was that solitary?

In any case, he was overloading her senses and she had to break free before she lost her mind entirely. Because on the short walk to the house, she'd wished they were out of sight long enough for her to ask for a do-over on his earlier kiss. One where she'd engage and respond by meeting him caress for caress instead of smashing his boys.

That longing was far more dangerous than some tiny crack in a bone.

And could hurt her way more.

She straightened her spine and tried to hold her chin up, though her face did hurt a bit, when she walked into the living room. She hugged her sister and then made the rounds of the entire Powertools crew, belatedly saying hello and thanking them again for all they'd done to prep the site for the event.

Joe, Eli's cousin, greeted her with a big old hug. He was good at them, making her feel safe and cared for even though she was clearly the third wheel...or fifteenth...in this arrangement. "Glad you're all right."

"Thanks," she murmured. "Now, where's that kid of yours? I want to see how big he's gotten. Cuter every time I see him on the videochat."

"Playing with Abby, where else?" He laughed as he jerked his chin toward the two toddlers causing a ruckus on the floor of the living room with a plastic workbench. Abby—Mike and Kate's daughter—held a giant red hammer while Nathan clutched a yellow screwdriver. They were giggling hysterically while banging at random. The floor, the toy, each other. They didn't discriminate.

Happy for an excuse to rest, Amber sank to the floor, her legs tucked to the side to accommodate her skirt. Abby rushed over and gave her a loud smacking kiss, transferring the hammer to Amber.

"For me? Thanks." She grinned until it hurt, adoring the little girl who was growing up surrounded by so much affection and adoration. What would it have been like to have that kind of support? If she ever had a family, she would want it to be like that.

Whoa. Where had that thought come from?

Amber had never considered herself the settling type. But it was hard not to be envious of the outpouring of love, sexiness, flirting and the more lasting loyalty she sensed every time she was around either the Powertools crew or her sister's own Hot Rods gang. Those bonds were responsible for these children—innocent and full of potential.

She wasn't sure she was up for the wild sexcapades of those groups—the sharing and everything—since she tended to be a lot more possessive and jealous than her sister, but the idea of an extended family...well, that was growing on her.

Good thing she was going to have a niece or nephew to spoil in a few months, huh?

Nathan stood up long enough to pile into her lap too. Instead of giving her his screwdriver, he pointed it over her shoulder. "Unc Gav. Play."

Great. Matchmaking kids too? Couldn't she catch a break?

Apparently not.

She looked up in time to see Tom and her mother grinning, along with Morgan, Sally and Devon, who gossiped over glasses of wine. Some of the guys had wandered into the kitchen or maybe onto the deck to grill dinner. Those who were left seemed to be entirely too interested in a couple of kids playing for her peace of mind. The last thing she needed was a bunch of rumors or speculation.

Well, actually...the *very* last thing she needed was to give in to the open invitation Gavyn had issued. A wedding affair was worse than a wedding hookup. She refused to be the desperate older sister of the bride. Even if a whole bunch of parts of her were voting in favor of no-strings release at the moment.

It'd been a crazy day, full of adrenaline and scary moments that drove her to seek reassurance. She refused to let herself cave to nature.

Still, when Gavyn sat beside her, it was hard to ignore the long, thick thighs that tucked against her or how enormous his hands looked when he cupped the baby's toy and showed him how to twist the matching plastic screws into the holes made for them.

Overall, he was gentle and kind despite his asshole tendencies.

Exactly the kind of man she stayed far away from. One that tempted her to try things she should know better than to devour like her cravings for dark chocolate ice cream despite her lactose intolerance. She'd pay for that indulgence.

Occasionally, it was worth some suffering.

Amber snuggled Abby, rocking her and nuzzling her soft baby hair for a while longer before the dread inspired by her mile-long to-do list overshadowed her joy.

"I'd better get to work." She set Abby down and got to her feet, looking around for her tablet.

"I put your things in your cabin," Dave told her. "Sorry, I didn't realize you were planning to do stuff tonight. Maybe you should take a break given the—"

"I can't." She cut him off then winced. "Sorry, I don't mean to be rude. There's still a lot to get done. I have to edit the programs and print them tonight so the vellum has time to dry before I assemble them tomorrow. I also need to unpack the crates from the bus and sort them so I can hit the ground running in the morning."

"I'll get the boxes for you," Gavyn said quietly from where he'd come up behind her. "You're not supposed to exhaust yourself while you're healing, remember?"

Dave glanced at her with wide eyes. "Is it worse than you said? I know a thing or two about recovering from an accident. Don't push yourself or you'll make it worse."

"It's nothing like what you went through." Amber couldn't help herself from squeezing the giant man. Imagining someone as tall and strong as him mangled and unable to fend for himself was nearly impossible. Or at least it would be if it weren't for his pronounced limp and the cane he sometimes still used.

"Still, I'm going with Gavyn on this one. There are a shit ton of dudes around here with nothing to do except shoot the shit and play video games. Let us help. We'll have it taken care of in no time. You just direct."

Gavyn stared at her until she relented. "Okay, fine."

"As soon as dinner is done," Dave promised.

She nodded, her rumbling stomach reminding her that she'd worked through lunch.

Despite her inner boss clamoring at her to get down to business, Amber couldn't deny that she enjoyed every second of huddling around the giant fire Mike, James, Eli and Holden built for them in the stone pit at the center of the deck while they devoured burgers, hot dogs and homemade potato salad. Being full didn't prevent her from finishing off the meal with the most delicious strawberry shortcake ever, courtesy of Morgan and her bakery, Sweet Treats.

Content and stuffed, she sat around for five more minutes. When she shivered, Gavyn scooted closer and draped his leather jacket over her shoulders. It was warm and smelled amazing. Like man and the mountain air that had rushed over them as they wound their way up to the resort earlier.

From her other side, her sister winked at her before nuzzling into Kaige's chest, where she was smothered in his embrace. It did feel sort of nice not being the only solo attendee.

Even Quinn had Buster, her mom hung out with Tom, and Abby played with Nathan.

Roman sat beside Gavyn, and they kept talking as if it were no big deal that he had made it his business to care for her. Maybe she was overreacting. Or at least that's what she thought until she peeked around the fire and found her mother staring intently at the spot where Gavyn's hand rested on her shoulder. Huh. When had that happened?

Amber shook her head no at her mother, hopefully subtly enough that no one else noticed in the commotion of their sidebar conversations, storytelling and general socializing. No one but Sabra, who had her camera pointing in Amber's direction. Oh jeez.

That was as much as she could handle.

"Sorry to be the buzz-kill, but I've got to get those boxes. You guys stay here and catch up." She knew how rare it was that the gaggle of friends got to see each other, never mind simply enjoy each other's company.

"Like hell," Gavyn growled at her.

In the end, he was right. What would have taken her close to two hours took the Hot Rods and Powertools together less than ten minutes. Plus it resulted in an impressive display of muscle that the women fully appreciated.

"This was a great idea," Morgan whispered conspiratorially to Amber. "Maybe tomorrow it will be hot enough for them to work with their shirts off. Something to consider."

She couldn't help but chuckle.

Thinking about all they had yet to accomplish made her realize she still had to finalize the programs. Besides, Tom and her mother had already headed off to their separate though adjoining cabins, taking Quinn and Buster with them.

So when the rest of them went back toward the fire pit, Amber knew she would only be intruding on the private time they probably wanted to spend together. For whatever...*stuff*...they had planned. Or some spontaneous revelry, she supposed.

"I'm heading to my bunk," she announced.

"Come on. I'll walk you." Gavyn took her elbow and she didn't have the energy to shrug him off. Not when the warmth of his hand and the stability he lent her were so comforting.

"Night, sis!" Nola blew kisses and waved along with the rest of their friends.

"See you tomorrow," Amber called back before wandering away, still smiling.

For a while, they strolled along the moonlit path in silence. She was glad for Gavyn's quiet company, realizing that although there were motion sensitive lights that illuminated her way as she approached, it was still a hell of a lot darker out here than she was used to in Middletown. Plus, it was a mountaintop. With bears and bats and who knew what else roaming around.

Obviously familiar with the grounds, he steered her unerringly toward their cabins, suspiciously next door to one another. *Thanks, Kayla.*

Gavyn broke the silence when they crossed a small bridge made of planks with no handrails. "This is one of my favorite spots. Want to sit, just for a minute? I feel like I should say something about what happened...before."

"That's not necessary," she said.

"Okay, then let me show you this because I want to." He tugged her arm and she didn't resist, curious about what could be better than the lovely flower beds they'd already passed or the glorious view of the lake she knew would be visible off to their right once the sun rose.

When he led her to a koi pond covered with netting, she asked, "What is this? Something to keep the birds from eating the fish?"

"Maybe it does that too." He grinned. "But no, it's a giant hammock. Take your shoes off so you don't drop them in. I heard Neil giving Dave shit about losing his engagement ring for Kayla in here when he proposed."

She laughed as she thought about that. "I guess that's a hazard you don't have to consider much at a naturist resort, huh?"

"Probably not." He chuckled with her, the sound low and sexy as hell. "I'm willing to try it and see if you want to get naked."

"Chilly tonight for that, I think." She refused to blush at his teasing.

"I'd keep you warm, Amber." He sounded dead serious.

"I already have your jacket," she reminded him.

"There are much better ways."

"Why are you doing this?" she asked as she crawled to the middle of the netting and lay face down to examine the flashes of gold made by the fish circling below them. Gorgeous. Mesmerizing. She could stare at them for hours. Some of the tension leeched from her.

"Hitting on you?" He stretched out beside her, resting his stubbled chin on his stacked forearms. "Because you're fucking hot. That's not news to you, is it?"

She laughed. "Whatever. Nola got the looks in the family. I mean, I'm okay, but come on. Is it because of all these freaking couples?

Does it mess with your mind to be the only one not part of a pair... or trio...or more?"

"Sounds like that's a question for yourself, love. Not me." He shifted until they were pressed together from toes to hips to shoulders.

"Or wait..." A horrible thought occurred to her. "You don't...you know...with them. Do you?"

"Gross, Amber. And see my kid sister naked and getting it on? I don't think so." He grimaced. "That's a boner killer for sure."

"I have the same problem, you know?" She grinned at him.

"You can't get a hard-on when you're around the Hot Rods because of your sister? Seriously?" His faux-shock had her laughing until tears formed at the corners of her eyes.

But when she peeked over at him, he'd gone serious.

"You're gorgeous, Amber. And I've been really impressed by the things I've heard about you from Kay."

"I think she's laying it on a little thick." Amber wiggled her fingers, wishing she had some food to sprinkle into the pond for the fish below. They broke the surface, enticed by her idle movements. "And...I don't know. I thought I was immune to their flirting and innuendos and the latent attraction always humming around the Hot Rods in general."

"But you're not?" he wondered.

"Maybe it's just too much with the crew too. Hell, how many of them are there between the two groups? Twenty? Even my mom and Tom are giving each other googly eyes. It's enough to make a girl..."

"Horny?" he supplied in what sounded like a hopeful tone.

"Lonely."

"Ah, shit." He paused as if weighing the merits of being honest in his quest to spend more personal time with her. Then he admitted, "Yeah, it makes me feel that way too sometimes, though I know they don't mean it to. Besides, truth is, I'm more traditional when it comes to sex, I guess. Maybe I'd experiment some, but I tend to limit my indiscretions to the standards—drinking, drugs and wild women to excess."

Those were not comforting thoughts. She knew he wasn't exaggerating either. After all, he'd met Roman in rehab. People could change—Barracuda was living proof of that—but so far, Gavyn seemed to be struggling. What if she did something to set him back?

Unintentionally, of course.

It was too much responsibility.

While she worried her lip, he stroked her hair, tucking the strands that had fallen forward behind her ears, then petting her from her crown to the middle of her back where her straightened locks fell in gentle waves. After several circuits, he whispered, "Amber, I'm not out here with you tonight simply because you're the only other unattached loser in the bunch."

She snorted. "Gee, thanks."

"There could be a hundred other women partying over there and I would still be trying to hook up with you. There's something about you..."

"Is that what you're doing?" She cut him off before he could say something he didn't mean simply to impress her. He didn't have to. The maddening caresses through her hair were doing a fine job of promoting him to her libido as it was.

"Oh, sorry. Was I supposed to hide my nefarious intentions from you?" He turned his face toward her and she mirrored him, staring into his light eyes, wondering what they would look like in the daylight this close up. Golden and gorgeous, probably.

"Nah." She shrugged. "You weren't very subtle, and I don't like liars anyway. I'd rather have things out in the open. That doesn't mean I'm going to give in. You don't understand how it is with me."

"Let me guess...complicated." He sighed.

"Yep." She laughed softly.

"Figures." Gavyn let his arm drape over her, and she didn't fling it off. It felt too nice. "That makes me feel better, though, love. I'm no simple man myself. I'm kind of a shitty bet, but I'd do for a couple nights."

"Ringing endorsement of yourself there, Gav." She cracked up and turned onto her side, suddenly more fascinated by him than the fish below.

He shrugged. The humor had fled from his face, erasing the crinkles at the corners of his eyes and mouth. She brushed her thumb over the spot, sad to see them go. "Honestly, Amber, I'm kind of freaking out."

"Why?" She tipped her head.

"Do you know how much booze is at a wedding?" He licked his lips. "Plenty."

"We can change that. No one will mind. I was already concerned for Roman. I'm sorry I didn't think that through." She winced.

"How about we come up with a different strategy? One where you keep me distracted? Be my date." He frowned. "Unless that's too much like babysitting..."

"No." She put her hand on his cheek and thought of the way he'd held her hand at the doctor's office earlier. "I'd love to go with you. Besides, I already did the seating chart. We're next to each other to make the table counts even since we're the only singles in the bunch. Why fight it, huh?"

He laughed, some of the fire returning to his gaze. "Wouldn't want to make more work for you, rearranging everyone."

They lounged together, watching each other as they settled. After his breathing seemed shallower and more steady, he asked, "Roman was really okay with the alcohol? He's fucking amazing. I don't know how he does that."

"You're doing a great job too, you know? It's not easy for him, but he loves Carver and I think, finally, he might be learning to say the same about himself. Those things give him the strength to resist. I can't imagine what it was like to grow up like he did, with an abusive parent. My mom might have checked out for a while after my dad died, but she'd never hurt us on purpose. It's no wonder Barracuda learned to rely on alcohol to numb the pain."

"See, that's the thing." Gavyn turned his face away. He rolled to his back and studied the stars with his hands behind his head. "I've got no excuse. My parents were sort of indifferent. They never lifted a hand to us or did anything other than provide their best for us. No one else in my family is an alcoholic that I know of. I know they say it's genetic, but who the hell gave me this disease? And why can't I cure it?"

Amber had no idea if she was equipped to answer him in the right way, but she knew when someone needed reassurance. So she gave it. She tucked herself against Gavyn, resting her head on his chest and tugging his jacket over them until it covered both of their torsos. "All we can do is our best, and it sounds like you're doing that. We can't always change who we are. I guess that's why you make me uncomfortable."

"Huh? Me?" He looked over at her, close enough now to kiss her again if he wanted. "How?"

"As I'm sure you noticed, I have a thing for order. For predictability." She sighed.

"I believe the term you're looking for is *control freak*, love." He softened the criticism with a soft buss of his lips on the tip of her nose.

"If you want to go that far." She had to try not to smile when she pulled out her feigned disbelief. "I can't put you in any box. You're crazy and kind. Sexy and arrogant. Outrageous and understanding. And when you call me 'love' it almost sounds like you have a British accent, which is ridiculously hot."

"That internship in London is finally paying off, then. So what you're saying is that I'm driving you nuts?" He sounded far too happy about that.

"Exactly."

"It's a start." He hummed. "Not bad for day one. Just wait until you see what I bring to the game tomorrow."

Amber would have laughed, except just then he rolled, pinning her beneath him. He stretched her hands above her head and captured her wrists in one of his palms. She had no intention of escaping, though, when he lowered, imprinting himself along every inch of her that was suspended over the garden oasis.

"May I kiss you, Amber?" His wicked grin belied his formality.

"If you don't, I might knee you in the nuts. Again."

Their laughter blended as he descended and took control of her smile. He plied it with bold strokes of his tongue and nips of his teeth before discovering what happened when they fused more completely. He swiped the roof of her mouth and along her tongue, swallowing her sighs, which threatened to shatter the stillness of the evening air.

When he'd stolen every last molecule of air from her lungs and made her woozy with desire, he lifted off and backed away, sitting on his heels as he sucked in breath after breath.

"You've got work to do, don't you?" He held out his hand to her.

"What happened to your evil plan..." Maybe it had run off with her resistance.

"For tonight, I want to pretend I'm one of the good guys." He shrugged.

Amber scooted off the net and got to her feet. When Gavyn joined her, she rose onto her tiptoes and gave him a chaste kiss on the lips before whispering, "You are, Gavyn. You are."

CHAPTER FOUR

At precisely seven o'clock the next morning, Gavyn balanced a tray of steaming coffee and a heaping breakfast for two, which he'd whipped up with the help of his sister, on one hand to knock on the door to Amber's cabin. It'd been worth Kayla's knowing grin to secure a hot meal that wouldn't poison their hardworking guest. He figured it might earn him a few bonus points if he saved her a trip to the main house when she would no doubt be eager to dig into whatever project it was she had planned first.

Hell, he'd spied the light on in her cabin well after 3am while he'd tossed and turned, mentally building a case for why he should stay put instead of kicking down her door before convincing her to let him fuck her senseless. The willowy shadow she'd cast on the thin curtains hadn't bolstered his defense to his stiff cock.

This time it was his head he banged on the door, while waiting for her to answer.

Though it would be even better if he was about to eat breakfast in bed with her, he looked forward to sharing a quick meal before diving in to the day.

He couldn't believe he was actually excited to work on wedding shit. With her.

"Yo, Amber! Are you in the shower or something?" Gavyn set the tray down and leaned over the porch railing to peek in her window. It was dark inside.

Oh, shit. Had he gauged her wrong? Was she actually getting some rest, like the doctor had prescribed? He frowned at the food growing colder by the second.

"You're wasting your time," Joe, who was walking past with his cousin, Eli, and his uncle, Tom, called from the path that meandered through this clump of cabins.

That was probably the truth. But Gavyn couldn't give up on the spark he'd felt from the first moment he'd spotted Amber or the passion she'd given him a hint of when they'd kissed the night before. Embarrassed, he abandoned his lame offering at her door and jogged over to the three men.

"Does she have a boyfriend?" Gavyn couldn't stop himself from asking when he got to them. That might explain her reactions, as if almost guilty about wanting him in return. He knew she did. It was a lot easier to read a woman when you weren't drunk off your ass apparently.

Plus, Kayla had been nudging him toward the sexy planner for weeks. That didn't mean she knew the details of Amber's personal life. Not as well as Eli would. The Hot Rods didn't keep anything from each other and Nola certainly had the dirt on her sister's love interests.

"Huh? No." Cobra shook his head. "But she's been up for a couple hours already. Sabra saw her go for a jog while she was doing yoga at the ass crack of dawn."

"She came over to the workshop to borrow some tools to install stuff at the pergola around six," Joe added.

Gavyn practically snarled. He bet she hadn't crashed at all. Yet she'd given him some lame-ass start time as if he couldn't handle an early beginning.

"Can I tell you what I'm seeing here?" Tom asked.

"Why not?" Gavyn kicked a rock. It bounced off the bark of a tree.

"Amber's not the kind of woman used to accepting help, never mind asking for it." Tom waved his hands in front of his chest. "She's tough, and she's not going to be very happy about you storming in here and trying fix her problems for her. If she won't even let her sister—or the rest of the Hot Rods gang— lend a hand, what makes you think she'll allow you to?"

"Because I'm just some drifter asshole with nothing better to do, not someone who matters. Definitely not someone she's trying desperately to gift a dream wedding to." Gavyn shrugged.

"I don't agree with that assessment, but...if you want any chance at convincing her before you put her hackles up or scare her off, you're going to have to change your tactics. Everything should seem like it's her idea. Let her see how much she's doing for you. Make yourself vulnerable, and *maybe* she'll do the same." Tom smiled kindly, as if he knew how difficult that would be for a man who wasn't used to letting anyone in.

Hell, some of the women Gavyn fucked hadn't even known his name. By comparison, Amber already surpassed everyone he'd been intimate with. And wasn't that sad? "I'll give it a shot."

Didn't seem like his usual methods were getting him very far.

"Good luck, kid."

"Thanks. See you guys around." He hung his head as he headed back to the porch to reclaim the tray.

As they drew away, Eli ribbed his dad. "If you're so damn smart when it comes to women and relationships, how come you aren't walking down the aisle with Ms. Brown this week, huh?"

Gavyn could relate to Tom's exasperated grunt in response. Food in hand, he took off toward the platform that held the elaborate structure Amber had designed.

He had admired the four-sided archway as the crew had constructed it the past few weeks, even helped some with the easy shit like hauling in supplies. The open-air formation didn't block the scenery while making an impressive spot for a significant occasion beneath the lattice dome at the center. It looked like it had always been there, yet enhanced the natural beauty of the resort.

After this, Kayla planned to make weddings a regular offering at Bare Natural. They'd be a hit once people got word of the improvements and saw the photos of this week's affair. He already knew it was going to be spectacular. Not to mention a ridiculous moneymaker.

This time, when he rounded the bend leading to the ceremonial marker, he slowed, acting as if he just happened to wander by. He didn't even say good morning until Amber looked up and spoke first. "Oh, Gayvn. Hi."

"Hey, yourself," he mumbled, trying for a tone about ten billion times more casual than he felt when he saw her again. In a thin, light blue sweater that hugged the curve of her breasts and the dip of her waist, she nearly made him trip over his own feet. The pair of jeans that left hardly anything to his imagination wasn't bad either. Every molecule in his body stood at attention and buzzed faster with her nearby. The rush was like one he'd gotten from the strongest shot of espresso he'd ever slammed in his courtroom days, or even the high that came after snorting a couple lines of coke. He was afraid he could get addicted to her. "Mind if I sit and eat?"

"It's not my place." She shrugged with a hint of a mile. "Do whatever you want."

"Careful what you ask for." He thought of the wicked things he'd like to attempt. If it were up to him, he'd have her stripped and kneeling in the soft grass in the next heartbeat, to hell with his absurd fantasy of remaking himself into someone decent.

They were both quiet for a bit as he perched on the wooden stairs that led to the square platform under the arches, then shoveled half of the omelet and hash browns into his face. He chomped down harder than necessary as he watched her in his peripheral vision. She lugged stuff around and climbed to the top rung of the ladder before standing on her tiptoes—precariously perched—to drill in a metal bracket for what looked like a curtain rod.

When it was either bite his tongue off or say something, he asked, "Want me to get the rest of those?"

"You don't think I can handle this by myself?" She didn't bother to look at him as she rearranged the supplies under the next location.

Warning. Warning. Danger. Warning!

Gavyn considered the advice Tom had given him and reformulated his approach.

"That's not it, Amber. I don't doubt that at all. But, you know, it's not like I got the Hot Rods a wedding present or anything." He tossed it out, casual-like. "If you let me do this with you—contribute to the effort—I'll feel less like a slacker who's always mooching off my sister and her friends."

His fingers gripped his thigh so hard he swore he was leaving bruises. Saying things out loud that he'd only visited in the dark of night as he berated himself, especially to a woman he was insanely attracted to, was tougher than he'd thought. Her judgment wouldn't just sting. It might crush him. And he had nothing to numb the pain.

Gavyn set aside the tray and stood, slowly approaching Amber, who'd made it down again in one piece.

Instead of arguing, she paused. She chewed on her lower lip for a few seconds while he stood there, with his hands jammed in the pockets of his jeans. When he prepared himself to walk away and let it go for good, she nodded. "Okay."

"Seriously?" Score one for Mr. London.

"Yeah, you're taller. I'm having some trouble reaching these." She grinned as she tossed him the drill.

"I've been told I'm a pretty good screwer," he boasted.

"Don't make me change my mind." She crossed her arms though her gorgeous smile still lit up her face, despite the slightly-less-puffy bruise she'd pretty successfully covered with makeup. "Just for that, I'm stealing some of your eggs while you're installing those brackets."

"Have at it." He didn't dare let her see his triumphant smirk as he climbed the ladder and got to work. The click of her fork against the plate filled him with ridiculous levels of satisfaction. And when she licked cinnamon sugar from the toast off her thumb, he thought he might howl.

"This is really terrific. Did Morgan cook it?" She spoke with her mouth full. He only took that as a second compliment.

"Actually, *I* did. With some help from my sister."

She got quiet again, making him afraid he'd blown his cover. So he ignored her and kept drilling holes. When he moved clockwise to the next arch, he'd built up a light sweat. Or maybe she'd done that to him. Either way, he stripped off his button-down shirt, keeping his black tank top in place.

Amber sounded like she might have choked when the muscles he'd defined lately came into view. Pride filled him, that his body could impress her. Still, he didn't acknowledge her unintentional praise, instead going back to work.

From there, he had a better vantage point from which to observe her scarfing down every last morsel on his plate. After she'd finished and wiped her mouth on the spare napkin he'd brought, she approached cautiously.

"I'm sorry we didn't talk about your shop last night." Amber rubbed her face then winced. "I owe you."

"You can make it up to me tonight." He thought of ways he could trick her into going to bed early instead. He must be sick or something, since as he schemed he was actually thinking of her catching up on her sleep instead of riding him. Well, no reason they couldn't do both.

He always slept better after great sex.

"There's not a lot of time..."

"Or after the big day. You're hanging around for the rest of the week, right? We'll make something work. Whenever." He shrugged. "I'm flexible."

A woman of her word, she nodded. Catching him off guard, she asked softly, "Will you tell me something?"

"Sure." He hoped he could honor that promise.

"How can you function like that? Going with the flow, I mean. Without rules? A schedule? A plan..."

He laughed. "It's been an adjustment. You know we're not *that* different, love."

"Oh yeah, how so?" She tipped her head and handed him the next set of screws so he didn't have to trek up and down the ladder again.

"Thanks." He brushed his fingers over hers as they transferred the hardware. "I'm a reformed tight-ass. A lawyer is really only someone who knows a bunch of rules and executes them. Or manipulates them to show his client was screwed over by someone who broke them. You can't be successful if you're not completely in line with those regulations, if you aren't familiar with them forward and backward. Even dumb shit like filing documents has to be done in a very precise manner. I'm a detail champ. Or was."

"Then why the change?" She offered him the first rod to snap into the brackets they'd installed. The work went faster as they kept each other company.

"I've found that those things only get screwed up and stress me out. So I've taught myself to take life as it comes. The counseling I went to in rehab helped some with that. You know, I spent every day surrounded by people who hated each other. They were vicious. Conniving. Cold. Hell, even my own parents split up. It didn't give me a lot of confidence in lasting relationships. Not only romantic ones or fuck buddies who have something more than a one-time thing, though I didn't tempt fate with those, but also friendships." He took a deep breath and prayed Tom was right. "I ended up isolated. With no outlet for my disgust, fear and frustrations other than another hit of something. To block it out, I guess. Who wants to live like that? I didn't. Don't. I think I was trying to end it all, subconsciously. I was so out of control."

He didn't realize he'd stopped installing her curtains until she was there, blinking up at him with huge, damp eyes. So he climbed down to talk to her face-to-face.

"I'm glad you weren't successful." She sniffled.

"Hey, if you're going to fuck up anything in your life, suicide-by-overdose is probably a great place to start." He tried to brush it off. His joke fell flat.

"What changed your mind? Made you want to try again?" Amber shocked him when she reached out first. Took his hand in hers and rubbed his knuckles with her thumb. He kept talking so she wouldn't stop touching him like that.

"I heard stories from Kayla, about the crew and how happy she was." He thought back on how he'd laughed at her at first. "I thought she was being naïve. Until I walked away from my job, shuttered my practice and said fuck it to pretty much everything I was responsible for. I came here and saw it for myself. So I checked into rehab."

"That's where you met Roman."

It wasn't a question, really, but he answered her anyway. "Yeah. When I did, he told me about Carver. The Hot Rods, too. And...I don't know. I guess I started to believe. But that was almost worse."

"How so?" She came closer, putting her hand on his chest.

"Because if that's true... If it's possible for people to love unconditionally and build someone up rather than tearing them down, even after a lifetime together, then I've wasted pretty much the entire time I've been alive. Took stupid chances. Checked out on the world for years, when I could have been looking for something a hell of a lot more meaningful."

He stared into her deep chocolate eyes as he confessed. Though he felt it, he didn't add that he could have been looking for someone who affected him like she did.

Attracted him like nothing except the promise of soaring on a killer high had before.

Then he laughed, aware he sounded crazy, because he was. "And if there's anything that'll drive a man to drink, it's overwhelming regret. So you see my problem, huh?"

"I know something about that and what it can do to a person, yes." She inched nearer, now putting her arms around his waist loosely as she laid her good cheek on his sternum. He hugged her back, glad for the contact. "Not mine, personally. Sort of. My mom blames herself for my father's death. He was killed when Nola and I were little."

Gavyn couldn't help himself. He began to rock her from side to side, almost as if they were slow dancing without music. "I'm sorry. That must have been horrible."

"It was a tragedy, but I'm not sure it was intentional. Sometimes shit just happens, you know?" She fisted her hands in the back of his onyx tank top. "She believes some people who had been harassing them drove him off the road. Because she's black, and he was white. And those fuckwads were ignorant."

"Son of a bitch." Gavyn suddenly felt like his issues were petty by comparison.

"You know what? Even if that's true, it's still not like it's her fault. She didn't ask them to harm him. She didn't preach hate or pass judgment about what kind of love is sacred and which is an abomination, as if any variety could be. It still didn't stop her from wasting decades of her life. Hell, she's about to blow her chance with Tom for something more." Amber sighed. "Sometimes I'm afraid I'm going to end up exactly like her because I don't know how to take chances. I never had the luxury of falling on my face considering my family was counting on me."

"You could try to let go of some of those rules now," he offered. "I'll help you up, if you'll do the same for me when I crash and burn. Maybe we'll both find out these missteps aren't fatal."

When confronted with the possibility, she backpedaled some, whipping out her bravado like a shield instead of wielding the genuine emotion she'd allowed him to glimpse moments before. "I'm not *that* afraid of failure."

"Fine. Prove it," he dared. "Take a risk. Do something impulsive. Unplanned. With me. Let's show ourselves that the world won't end if we do."

"Right now?" she squeaked.

"Kind of the definition of spontaneous." He chuckled. "I'll make it easy for you. Let go. I'll take care of you. I get the feeling no one's done that. Maybe ever. You were looking out for Nola, and yourself, and your mom. I get that. But, newsflash: Love, they're doing great. It's you who has them worried now. I could see it when we walked in last night."

"Because I'd just gotten in a car accident, that's all."

"It's part of it, of course. But not *all*. No." He shook his head. "They're concerned about you and how you're handling everything changing around you."

"Great. Now I've got to be more careful when I'm near them?" She wilted in his hold.

"Or you could be more honest," Gavyn said, recapping Tom's earlier advice to him. "Starting right now, with me. You want me, don't you? At least half as much as I want you, I'd wager."

She drew in a quick breath. Her nails dug into the muscles at his shoulders for a moment before she looked up and admitted it with a rueful twist to her perfect lips. "At least."

"Thank you," he moaned as he lowered his head and sealed their mouths together briefly. "So let me practice on you. This is a new thing for me too. Responsibility for someone else and their happiness. Giving a damn about my partner beyond supplying the fuck of a lifetime."

"It's so hot when you're modest." She laughed.

"Hey, I promised to be truthful." He flashed her a wicked grin. Because *this* he didn't doubt. He knew his way around a woman's body. No one had ever accused him of being a bad lover. "So, what do you say? Are you in?"

His heart slammed in his chest as he waited for her to leap with him.

"Yes," she breathed.

CHAPTER FIVE

In a flash, Gavyn spun, tucking them beneath the fall of the gauzy material they'd been adding to the structure for a more romantic effect. It worked. With Amber cocooned in yards of silk, she looked even more stunning than he had thought her before. The white fabric enhanced the mocha tone of her skin and made her appear exotic and extra vibrant by comparison.

He swallowed hard before leaning down and staring into her eyes. He could get lost in their depths, would love to watch her pupils dilate as he sank into her. That he would save for a time when he could do it right.

Gavyn backed Amber up until she leaned on one of the pergola's supports. He trapped her between the post and his body. She conformed to every plane of him, curves yielding where he was firm. His cock rivaled the four-by-four against her spine with its hardness.

Her breasts were lush compared to her lanky frame and made a perfect handful when he cupped her through her sweater and bra. His thumbs traced the hardened tips he could feel despite the barriers he wanted to strip from between them.

One step at a time.

Amber's head rolled from side to side as she surrendered to his touch. He paused to kiss her injured cheek with the barest of glances from his lips. She opened her eyes and smiled, though her lids seemed heavy with the lust coursing between them.

"How's that feeling?" he asked.

"Can't even tell it's there when you're looking at me like that," she admitted.

When he hesitated, soaking in the anticipation and electricity sparking between them, she attacked. Amber kissed her way down his neck, licking and biting him there in an explosion of animalistic passion that triggered every single one of his dominant male instincts.

Answering her with even greater fervor, he growled as he let his hands roam down her flat stomach, covered by the fuzzy sweater, to the waistband of her jeans. He tucked his fingers inside the denim to swipe at the sensitive skin just below her bellybutton, wishing she'd worn her skirt today instead.

Though, if she had, he might be tempted to spin her around, bend her at the waist and slide inside the moist heat between her legs.

He would fuck her from behind every bit as ferociously as she was begging him to with her show of aggressive ardor. Damn the fact that they were standing outside in broad daylight. Sort of.

Gavyn withdrew his fingers after teasing her a bit, then rotated his hand so he cupped her mound, holding her in his hand. He lifted, raising her to her tiptoes so that she was slightly off balance and loving every second. When she moaned, he quickly brought his mouth to hers and swallowed the cry. He kissed her while she responded to his every touch, arching against his squeezing fingers, undulating as though she needed release as badly as he longed to give it to her.

His lungs burned, forcing him apart from her lips the barest bit. He whispered, "Quiet, love. Not a sound."

For a moment she froze, her eyes darting this way and that in their flimsy shelter.

"No, I don't hear anyone. Yet. But I could. There could be people anywhere, any time. So be a good girl and do as I say. Let's put your inner control freak to good use, huh?" He pressed a soft kiss to the corner of her mouth while one hand came up to cup her chin, allowing his fingers to curl lightly around her neck. In awe, he watched as she quit fighting and surrendered to his will. Completely.

It was as if handing off the burden, relinquishing responsibility to him, turned her on even more. She shuddered in his grip.

"You like that?" He already knew the answer, since she had started grinding on his hand in a seductive figure eight. And when he didn't move, instead studying her and her glorious transformation, she reached for him.

"Hands behind your back," he ordered, and she complied. "Keep them there unless I tell you otherwise."

Amber nodded, though her eyes were closed, preventing him from seeing into her soul.

"You'll look at me when we fool around like this, love," he told her.

Dark lashes fluttered then held as she struggled to do as he commanded.

"Very good," he whispered into her ear, nuzzling her as his hand continued its maddening massage through her clothes. "For being so brave, I think you deserve a reward."

Her uneven breaths and low whine made it clear how she struggled to stay silent. To please him. She was made for this kind of sensual play. For him. Everything he enjoyed about sex seemed a hundred times more pleasurable when he was doing it with her. The chase. Conquering. Granting pleasure.

It would have been impossible for him to stop himself from giving her what she deserved then. With a flick of his hands, he unfastened the button on her jeans then drew down the zipper. His knuckles brushed the soaked triangle of her panties as he did.

Humming his approval, he lifted his fingers to his face long enough to draw a deep breath and the scent of her inside him, memorizing it. Only then did he suck on his fingers, getting his first taste of her unique flavor.

"Delicious," he murmured.

Amber slouched as pleasure overwhelmed her. He wrapped one arm around her, easily supporting her against his body as his other hand returned to her pants. Though the possibility of being discovered thrilled him, he didn't dare risk leaving her unfulfilled.

With less tact than she deserved, he tucked his fingers beneath the elastic of her panties, then began to trace the seam of her drenched pussy.

"Gavyn!" she cried out at the first touch.

He froze.

"What did I tell you about staying quiet?" he asked, thrilled for the excuse to pinch her clit, hopefully sending a shockwave of blended pain and pleasure through her. The intense sensations caused her knees to wobble and more of her weight to rest on his supporting arm.

"I will. Promise. Just don't stop," she begged, completely lost in the moment.

"You're still talking." He gave her his wicked grin, loving how she melted against him.

She bit her lip to keep quiet, spreading her legs wider and pressing herself into his palm. The physical request was even more alluring than her pleas had been.

Gavyn growled, dropping his forehead to hers as he continued where he'd left off. This time he used his middle finger to part her labia, then inserted it in one fluid glide that left his thumb perfectly positioned to rub her engorged clit.

By the time he'd added a second finger to her tight sheath and began to press forward in syncopated pulses while circling the bundle of nerves with the pad of his thumb, she'd begun to quake in his hold.

"Never imagined you'd be getting off with a near stranger where anyone could find you, did you, Amber?" He spoke so softly he could hardly hear himself. Still, he couldn't help stimulating her mind as much as her body. Maybe more.

She shook her head, as if refusing to risk him stopping if she uttered the admission.

"Good girl." Gavyn reclaimed her mouth as he thrust his steely cock against her hip. Too much rutting on her and he'd embarrass himself. No, he was saving that for when he was finally inside her. Her mouth or her pussy—hell, her tight ass for that matter—he didn't much mind where. "Sometimes it pays to break the rules."

The rings of muscle along her channel were clamping on his fingers as he scissored them within her now. She was so responsive. So smoking, he almost didn't want it to end. Neither would he torture her when she'd been audacious enough to experiment with him.

So he nestled closer to her, pinning her tighter to the post behind her as he impressed himself on every part of her he could reach. "Let me see how gorgeous you are when you come apart. Will you do that for me, Amber?"

Her mouth dropped open on a silent moan.

He took the opportunity to slide his tongue into the warm, moist space. He fucked her there in a reflection of his fingers inside her, swirling along the tip of her tongue in sync with the thrumming of his thumb on her clit. Still, he sensed she needed a tiny bit more to crest.

So he used one booted foot to kick her legs wider, putting her off balance and entirely in his grasp, relying on him to keep her from falling. As she relinquished control to him, she dropped a bit lower, grinding on his hand in the process.

Her eyes locked on his, her mouth forming an "O" as she hovered on the brink of ecstasy.

"That's right. Come for me, Amber," he whispered. "Come on my hand. Squeeze me tight inside you as you unravel."

She panted as she strained toward him.

"Let go. I've got you," he promised.

And she did.

Amber thrashed, her entire body spasming around him, drawing his fingers deeper into the lush paradise between her legs. Her pussy wrung his fingers, making him wish it was his dick being strangled instead of the digits.

Afraid he couldn't support her comfortably as she continued to come in his arms, he withdrew, hugging her to him, sheltering her against his chest. And when she'd recovered, just a little, he leaned her against the post, made sure she was stable, then knelt in front of her.

He quickly buttoned her pants, fixed her sweater and then rose, sliding his slick fingers into his mouth so she could watch him lick every drop of her arousal from them.

Tomorrow night, he would drink direct from the source.

They both knew it.

"Amber? Are you down here?" Ms. Brown called from somewhere entirely too close for comfort.

Gavyn quickly checked his own clothes, making sure he was presentable before giving Amber one last light kiss. Lips parted, eyes glazed, she looked thoroughly sated. It was sexy on her, but made it beyond obvious what they'd been up to.

So he murmured against her mouth, "Catch your breath. Settle down. I've got you covered."

He winked at her, then burst from behind the drapery. He spotted the now-empty breakfast tray and used it as the perfect excuse. Holding it in front of him to hide his raging erection, he set out to meet Amber's mom before she could round the last bend in the path and bust her daughter.

"Good morning, Ms. Brown," he said, acting as if he'd just finished breakfast and planned to return his used stuff up to the house.

"Hi, Gavyn," she practically purred with a mysterious smile. "Have you seen Amber?"

"Yes, we were hanging the drapery over here a while ago." Not a lie.

"But she's not there now?" Ms. Brown pointed.

He smiled as broadly as he could manage and evaded her question, relying on his legal training to get him through this cross-examination. "I'd be glad to come find you when she's got a second."

"Don't add to the things she's got on her plate today. I only wanted to make sure she's doing all right and that her cheek isn't any worse this morning. You saw her earlier, right? She's okay?" She tipped her head, her eyes narrowing as if warning him not to fudge the truth when it came to her daughter's wellbeing.

"Yes. It's bruised, of course, but she seems fine." He didn't have to lie about that. "I'd have taken her straight to the emergency room myself if I thought otherwise. I swear."

"Hmm." She nodded. "In that case, I'm about to be on babysitting duty with Tom for the rest of the afternoon."

"Have fun with Nathan and Abby." His smile was genuine when he thought about the tiny troublemakers.

Right before Ms. Brown turned toward the main house, she lowered her voice and murmured, "It'd be easier to believe your entire story if you didn't have lipstick down the side of your neck, son. A shade I know well, seeing as it's one I bought my daughter for her birthday. Go on back to her. Take your tray shield too. If you hurt her, you'll have to answer to me. And then her sister. And then the Hot Rods. Which would probably cause some Powertools versus Hot Rods feud, *West Side Story*-style. Nobody wants that. I wouldn't take that kind of chance if I were you."

"Wasn't planning on it, ma'am." He liked Amber's mom almost as much as he liked Amber herself.

"Good boy. So long as we understand each other." She patted his cheek twice, then turned on her heel without a backward glance.

Gavyn would have laughed if he wasn't terrified Amber would hear and freak out. He couldn't believe her mother had given him, fuck-up that he was, a seal of approval—even if it was a conditional one. Hey, he'd take that.

He sprinted back to where he'd left Amber and ducked under the material to find her sitting cross-legged with her head in her hands. Not exactly the state he'd left her in.

"You okay?" he crooned as he sank beside her.

When he reached out to cup her shoulder, she flinched from his grasp. What the fuck? "Amber? Are you crying, love?"

"Hell no." She lifted her head, letting him glimpse the fire there instead of the icy tears he'd expected. Whew, he could deal with that far easier. "I'm pissed."

"At me?" He winced. "Sorry, I should have taken you somewhere more private, where I could have done a better job."

"Don't be ridiculous," she snapped, only turning him on more with her fighting spirit. "I'm angry at myself. For getting distracted. For being selfish. Look at this mess. Half the morning's gone and I'm wasting time screwing off with you. Letting you boss me around instead of keeping my head on straight."

Ouch. That one stung.

"Funny. It didn't feel like a *waste* to me." He tried not to be offended or hurt. The truth was, he'd thought they were forging the beginnings of something special. To hear her dismiss their chemistry like it was common knifed him deep.

"I can't do this, Gavyn." She kept him at arm's distance as she climbed to her feet gracefully then systematically wiped the emotion from her face. "I've got a job to do. The most important moment of my sister's life is in thirty-one hours and twenty-seven minutes and I'm not about to disappoint her for the sake of an orgasm or two with a stranger. No matter how spectacular they are."

Well, he had that in his favor, at least.

"Stop talking, Amber." If she didn't, he was afraid he might cave to the part of his brain screaming at him to take off for the nearest bar. It was time to prove he'd meant what he'd told her earlier. "Obviously, I was wrong about us. About the timing. Or trying to experiment without guardrails. Fine. But that doesn't mean I'm going to leave you flat on your ass. I'm helping you with the wedding shit like I said I would. We'll get it done."

She blinked at him a few times. "You are? We will?"

"Fuck yes." He snarled, snatching her hand and pressing it to his still-hard cock. "And in approximately thirty-seven hours, or some shit like that, you won't have any excuses left. We'll deal with this then."

"Oh." She swallowed hard enough that he watched her pretty neck flex.

His grin was likely predatory, but he didn't give a fuck.

He followed it up with his best imitation of an innocent smile. "So, love, what's next on your list?"

CHAPTER SIX

Amber couldn't believe her baby sister was getting married. After months of preparation, today was the day. She sniffled to keep her makeup flawlessly preserved.

"You okay?" Gavyn came up behind her at the mirror. She liked the way they looked together. He'd shaved and put on an expensive suit from his prior life that looked like it had been cut exclusively for his well-muscled frame. It complemented the deep purple gown her sister had selected. It seemed a bit much for the sister-of-the-bride, but part of her was secretly thrilled Nola had insisted, considering Amber had never gone to her prom or any other formal event.

Especially since Gavyn couldn't stop staring at the things the sweetheart neckline did to showcase her boobs, which looked pretty great if she did say so herself. A black sash cinched her waist and long, decadent feathers trimmed the skirt where it flared out around her calves. She'd never felt so sexy, whether because of the dress or the man staring at her. Maybe both.

Even if they were exhausted. He'd stayed with her, working side-by-side, until every last detail was in order, only finally sacking out on the couch of her cabin not that long ago for what amounted to a cat nap instead of a full night's rest. Without hitting on her. Or even trying to sneak in a quickie, though she kind of wished he had so she would have had an excuse to be weak again. Yet he'd never once complained.

Somehow, sleepy looked a lot like sexy on him.

"Yeah," she answered softly as she allowed herself to lean back into his strong chest for a moment. "Just thinking about the times Nola and I dreamed of what this day would be like when we were girls."

"Princess outfits and unicorns?" he guessed.

"Pretty much, with some tiaras and glitter thrown in for good measure." She sighed, thinking of how far they'd come. Proud of what they'd built. "We didn't have fancy toys or a TV to watch, so we relied on our imaginations plenty during the times we shared a 'bedroom', also known as the backseat of Mom's van, when things got rough."

"Damn, Amber." He rubbed her bare arms lightly. The gentle up and down motion soothed her. "Is that why this is so important to you? Why you've been pushing yourself so hard?"

"I guess that's part of it, yes." She hadn't thought of it in those terms until he framed it that way.

"I'm not an expert in matrimonial shit, but I'd have to say, your setup looks amazing and I can't wait to eat everything on the menu you showed me. Seconds on the chocolate caramel cake. It's going to be a kick-ass party if nothing else." Though he never stopped smiling, his eyes flickered away from her for the tiniest instant. Given his ultra-intense focus on her every other time, it was obvious to her.

"You're worried about the reception? I don't want to torture you. Please, let me cancel the open bar. It's not too late. I have the caterer's number on speed dial." Amber turned in his loose hold, feathers floating around her ankles in the resulting breeze, and set her hands on his chest.

"I'm not going to ruin everyone else's good time. I'll be all right as long as I have you to distract me. I mean, you did see how fucking stunning you are when you were looking in that mirror, right?" He stole a quick kiss. One that had her toes curling in her black stilettos. Even with the high heels, he still had her beat in height, not something most guys could say. "I can't wait to unwrap you from this dress tonight."

Neither could she. Still, she didn't want to drop their conversation like that, distracted by the promise of pleasure. "If you change your mind about the bar..."

"I won't. Don't worry." He trailed one fingertip along the top edge of her bodice, over the swells of her breasts. "You're a lot more tempting to me right now."

She could relate.

"I want to taste you even more than that cake, and I've been dreaming about that since we placed the order four months ago." Amber licked her lips.

"You're killing me, love." The muscle in his jaw flexed and suddenly she knew what she wanted to do for this guy, who'd made her last few days ones she would always remember fondly, hopefully more so after tonight. To return the favor from yesterday.

She glanced at her watch before sliding her hand down the row of buttons on his shirt to cup the bulge in the front of his pants, then murmured, "Well, we *are* seven minutes ahead of schedule, and I've always had this fantasy about blowing a man fully dressed in a suit."

His head dropped back and he groaned when she sank to her knees in front of him, deftly unbuckling his belt, opening his pants and lowering his zipper to fish for his cock while leaving the rest of his clothing undisturbed.

"Amber..."

She didn't want him to stop her or inject any reason into her brain that would prevent her from completing her mission. "Just shut up and let me suck you."

To his credit, he did.

He hissed when she used one hand to cup his balls, rolling them and testing their weight while the other wrapped around his thick shaft. God, he was...more than a handful. If he fucked like he fingered, she might not survive the night or she'd be ruined for other men after that.

Though that thought troubled her, making her wonder if she'd be able to forget him when she headed back to Middletown, she pushed away anything negative and embraced only the positive. For today, anyway, nothing could ruin her mood.

After she measured his length, stroking him from root to tip several times, he began to grow impatient. She liked that about him. How steadfast he was in his need for her. She'd never felt so desperately desired before in her life. This was no exception.

Gavyn curled his hand around the back of her neck and drew her closer. Her breath washed over the full head of his cock, which stood out in relief from his shaft. Imagining what that ridge would feel like inside her, stroking her in all the right places, made her shiver with anticipation.

Reaching out her tongue, Amber licked him along the prominent vein that decorated his underside. She paused to sip the bead of precome that appeared at his tip.

"Ah fuck." His thighs corded against her shoulders, making her smile. As she opened her mouth, he thrust his hips toward her, feeding her his cock. "Yes, that's it. Suck me, love."

Amber complied, giving them both what they wanted. She drew on him with steady pulls, working her lips lower along his impressive length, filling her mouth with his heat and hardness. Only the press of his blunt cap against her throat had her pausing, and then just long enough to allow herself to relax and accommodate him.

Pulling off a bit then working him back inside, she soon held all of him.

By the time she began to bob over his length, he'd started rocking to meet her.

"For the record," he groaned, "I can last a lot longer. Don't. Want. To make you late."

She laughed around him, causing him to grunt and press deeper on their next pass. Hoping he understood that she wanted to destroy him as rapidly and completely as he had done to her the day before, she grabbed his tight ass and yanked him to her. She swallowed around his length, letting her tongue dance across the sensitive spot below his tip.

And within moments, he cursed. His shaft jerked and he started to warn her, "I'm gonna—"

Amber took that as her cue to suck harder, stroke him faster.

He roared as he came, releasing a stream of warm fluid that she drank in sip after sip until he had nothing left to give her. Neatly, she tucked him in and put his clothes back in order. Though his chest bellowed and his cheeks were red, he helped her to her feet and hugged her tight before murmuring, "Thank you."

Then he kissed the shit out of her.

Though she could have stood there making out with him for the rest of the week, he drew away with a sigh then spanked her

hard enough to make her jump. "Get ready. We've got to leave in ninety seconds or so."

Amber laughed, but knew he was right. Too bad because that appetizer had only made her hungrier for the real thing.

As she rounded up the last of her belongings, she noticed Gavyn staring at his crotch. Had she hurt him? Was he still horny? She thought she'd done a pretty fantastic job of sucking him dry...

"What are you doing?" she couldn't help but ask.

"Making sure there's no lipstick on my pants." He grimaced. "Your mom would *definitely* notice that. I don't need her calling me out in the middle of the ceremony or sic'ing Tom London on me or something. He's still a beast, for an older dude."

Amber laughed so hard tears threatened her mascara. Sometime after midnight, he'd confessed about her mother's threats and her keen eye for detail. It didn't bother her. She'd never be able to hide her affair with Gavyn from either her mom or Nola. Not that she wanted to anyway.

Her cheek ached, though she suspected it was more from how happy Gavyn made her than the lingering bruise there. When she yanked the door open, armed with her tablet, copies of the vendor contracts, a timeline, the reception speech she had memorized and emergency contacts, she froze.

What were those clouds doing over there, looking dark and ominous?

"No. No, no, no." She stopped dead and Gavyn bumped into her backside.

"Forget something?" He kissed her neck.

"I checked the weather forecast every day for the last month. It's never once showed a hint of rain." She shrieked, "What is that?"

"There are some things you can't control, love," Gavyn reminded her. "No one's going to blame you if the weather doesn't cooperate."

"That's *not* an option." She put her hand on her hip then took off for the main house.

Wisely, Gavyn didn't speak to her as they speed-walked, as fast as she could manage in her crazy get-up, to the main house. Kayla and Dave had offered to let the brides get ready there, together, for their special day. They'd already been at it for a couple hours, according to the texts she and the other ladies had exchanged this morning when she'd pinged them to confirm they were on track.

When they reached the cabin, she stormed up the stairs and burst through the door.

"Wow. What's up?" Sabra asked. She looked perky and fashion-forward in the short blue dress that accentuated her fine

Asian features. A longer, gauzy, polka-dotted section in the back created the illusion of a full-length gown and train. It was exactly her style.

"I hate to tell you this. All of you. But...have you seen the sky?" Amber's brows drew together and her frown tugged at her sore cheek.

"Kinda sucks," Carver said from the kitchen, where he was eating some kind of breakfast sandwich.

"First of all, what are you doing in here?" The grooms had their own designated area. If she didn't know where people were, things were going to get off track quickly.

"Hey, I'm pretty much a bride, right?"

"No. Not at all," she corrected. "Secondly, what do you mean *kinda* sucks?"

"Well, I'd hoped we'd get to use the pergola the crew built and the rest of that fancy shit you set out yesterday. The plants and chair coverings and everything looked really cool. Not likely that's going to happen. So the guys moved the chairs under the reception pavilion, just in case." He shrugged, seeming more concerned about the bacon he dropped on his shirt not making it to his mouth than the mark it would leave behind on his formalwear or that his entire wedding day might be ruined.

"They disassembled my setup?" She was a few heartbeats away from a panic attack.

"Um, yep." He kept talking, one leg crossed over the other, ignoring the women waving their hands over their heads like aircraft controllers behind Amber's back. "We can redo it if the sun comes out. Didn't take more than a half hour. Definitely not as pretty as how you had it, since it's kind of squished onto the dance floor under the tent, but, eh, it'll do."

"I can see your reflection in the damn window, Nola," she barked at her sister. "Why stop him now? Tell me what else is screwed up, Carver."

"Oh. Shit." Meep looked from her face, which had to be stormier than the sky outside, then to her sister and their friends before making good on his nickname. "Well, uh, I think my phone is buzzing. Probably Roman. You know, with groom stuff. Gotta go."

Then he flew out the door, sandwich still in hand, saving himself from a freshly ripped asshole.

Amber felt her teeth click together as they chattered. She was tired and on edge. This could not be happening. Gavyn stepped aside right when she needed to lean on him most. It would have hurt her if she hadn't realized

Nola was squeezing between them to surround her in a gentle hug.

"Amber, I love you." Her sister stayed that way for a while then retreated, rubbing her noticeable baby bump. "I appreciate everything you've done to make today wonderful for me and the rest of the Hot Rods. But honestly, we have the important stuff already. Our friends and family are here. We've got food and music and each other. Today is a celebration, yes. Rain or no rain, we're going to enjoy every minute. So please, don't worry or spend an instant of it being upset. That's the absolute last thing I want."

Gavyn put his hand on Amber's shoulder and squeezed. Could he know that her heart was shriveling, wondering if all her effort had been for nothing? Either because it would be ruined or because it didn't actually matter to anyone except her at the end of the day.

Nothing like feeling useless.

Especially when she'd spent her whole life taking care of her sister, trying her best to help Nola survive, aiming for them both to be happy. In reality, the spectacular woman her sister had grown into hadn't needed Amber for anything in a very long time. Now, she was officially out of a job.

At least the man holding her hand seemed to have some ideas on how she could spend her free time. For the next few days, at least. Then what? When she packed up and went back to Middletown, where would that leave them?

A fun memory, she supposed. Possibly the only one from this disastrous event.

"Come on, sis." Nola waved toward the living room. "Why don't we keep on your schedule and hope it blows over? No use getting upset for nothing, right?"

"Sure." Amber smiled her best fake smile and went to check out the other gorgeous brides in their distinctive gowns. They truly did look lovely. Kaelyn wore a more casual, though no less dazzling, hand-painted silk gown covered in a riot of wildflowers. Nola had on the flowing lavender dress with a beaded crystal bodice and an empire waistline she'd fallen in love with the first time she tried it on.

They were stunning and unique.

Amber couldn't help herself. She diverted toward the window to curse the skies for taking anything away from the three beautiful friends and their five handsome grooms.

***

Two hours later, Amber stood at the floor-to-ceiling windows in the main house, watching rain pour in streams down the panes. They were supposed to be taking group portraits in the flower gardens as of fifteen minutes ago. Hope of that happening had vanished.

She glanced down at her phone and updated the radar once more. It seemed like a cluster of rogue clouds were parked directly above Bare Natural. If they would just scoot out of the way...

Of course, she'd been thinking that very thing for the past hour and a half.

So at first she thought she was imagining it when the rain came slower and slower.

In the distance she spotted blue skies. Limning the edge of them and growing stronger and stronger, sunlight pierced the gloom.

Gavyn squeezed her hand, his fingers entwined with hers as they had been since she'd taken up watch over the storm. "Hey. It's breaking up, love."

She turned to him with a mammoth smile, but when she faced the room she found no one else looking except her. The rest of the guests were laughing, snacking on the finger foods the caterers had set out, talking and generally enjoying their time together. Decked out in their snazziest clothes, they lounged around the log cabin as if it were the posh surroundings she'd precisely arranged for today's festivities.

How much had she missed out on with her back turned in the pursuit of perfection?

Deep in her gut, she felt something shift, and realized that everyone was right. Nola, her mom, Gavyn...

She had to learn to let some of this go.

After today.

Amber raised her voice. "Everyone, I think we have a shot. If you want to do this outside, let's give everything an hour to dry out and we'll start the ceremony."

Not too much later than they'd planned, either. Sure, she'd have to move to Plan B for the pictures. The rest could be salvaged, she'd bet.

The wedding party sounded off in agreement.

Amber went back to work. This time she focused on how to get her friends married rather than creating some storybook vision. Fortunately for the Hot Rods, her excessive preparations meant they'd have both.

CHAPTER SEVEN

Gavyn had attended quite a few weddings. Guys from law school getting hitched, former clients remarrying—usually to the people they'd cheated on their spouses with—and even one he'd crashed when he'd followed some hot chick in a pretty dress to the ceremony she was a bridesmaid in. Usually the only thing he liked was the free liquor.

Somehow this was different.

He stood beside Roman, Carver and Quinn under one of the four arches that ringed the large pergola. Beneath each of the other ones was another of the Hot Rods couples tying the knot. In the center, a diverse group of friends and family sat in a circle. As the focus switched from couple to couple, they turned their seats ninety degrees.

Amber really had made a potentially awkward situation into something spectacular and inimitable, like the people pledging themselves to each other that day.

Gavyn stared at her, directly across from him, where she attended her sister.

As if she could feel his gaze, she met it with her own warm stare and smiled.

It was as though trouble had lifted from her soul at the same time the rain had vanished, leaving behind the boldest rainbow he'd ever seen. Sure, the gang had missed out on getting their photos taken in the gardens, but they'd ended up with a backdrop that couldn't be arranged or bought.

The pergola had sheltered them and been perfectly framed by the complete double arch of vibrant colors. The grooms had held umbrellas over their brides, adding another interesting element to the scene. The photographer had just about passed out with delight when he'd reviewed the shots on the display of his digital camera.

Probably figured he'd be booked solid for the next ten years at least when he added those images to his portfolio. Of course, Gayvn's favorite part had been the way he and Amber were paired up as the two solo attendees in the wedding party.

Knowing he'd have a memento of their time together sat well with him. Really well, although he wished he could cling to more of Amber than a photograph.

He tuned back in to the ceremony in time to hear the four couples reciting vows that left everyone reaching for the tissues Amber had included in the program packets at their seats. At the last moment, before the recessional music began, Amber announced to the crowd that the Hot Rods ladies had a surprise for their guys. Each of them revealed a matching shop logo tattoo, proclaiming themselves Hot Rods for life.

Gavyn knew the meaning went deeper than business. He was envious of the network of love and lust they had built. He wasn't greedy. If he could win a single woman's heart—one particular woman's—he thought he could be happy with that.

Roman elbowed him in the ribs. He looked directly at Amber, then back to Gavyn, and whispered, "You know, I'd be glad to return this favor someday."

"That might be a little premature. I haven't even gotten her to sleep with me yet." He tried to laugh it off. For the first time, a single hook up didn't seem like the end goal. Burying himself inside her once wasn't going to be enough. He already knew that.

"Good luck." Barracuda smirked. "I don't think you need it. She's giving you you're-going-to-get-lucky eyes."

"God, I hope so." He disguised his chuckle behind a faux-cough when Ms. Brown turned her head in his direction. She tipped the wide-brimmed purple hat that made her look like an old-Hollywood starlet so she could glare at him from the opposite side of the space, as if she had supersonic hearing. Or magical powers.

Like her daughter, who had cast some kind of spell on him.

With a dazzling smile, and maybe a hint of laughter, Amber watched him from across the room. Only the thunderous applause and whistles of the Powertools and Hot Rods not on display broke their connection. He realized the four couples were sharing their official first kiss.

Beside him, Roman had dipped Carver and was about to jam his tongue so far down his throat he licked the guy's toes. Impressive.

Gavyn whooped along with everyone else. Mostly because wrapping up here meant he got to spend time with Amber. Alone, eventually. He'd settle for dinner and dancing until then.

She rounded to his side of the pergola as the recessional went on and he fell into step beside her, offering his arm, which she accepted without hesitation.

"Congratulations." He kissed her cheek as they headed for the pavilion a little way down the path. Even the soggy grass looked dazzling, covered in raindrops. The fresh scent of spring filled the air. "I can't imagine how that could have gone any better. You did a fantastic job, Amber."

"Thanks." She smiled up at him. "At the end of the day, seeing them all so in love... Yeah. That's what counts. I kind of got lost for a while, I guess."

"You're on the right track now?" He held out her chair at their shared table.

"I could be." She leaned closer to whisper in his ear, "If you still plan to help me do something wild later."

"That can be arranged." He was so engrossed in her that it caught him off guard when the waiters circling hovered over his shoulder and offered them a tray of glasses. White wine on one side, red on the other. Without thinking, his hand reached for one.

Then jerked when Amber gasped, "Gavyn, no."

Awkward and ashamed, he froze with his fingers dangling in midair.

"Neither of us will be drinking tonight, thank you." She covered graciously for him as he fought the parched sensation in his mouth that begged the man to return and pour the entire contents of his serving dish down Gavyn's throat.

Blindsided, he wrestled with the powerful and uncontrolled urge.

Roman must have seen the whole incident. He stepped over with Carver and crouched beside Gavyn's chair, between him and Amber, while Meep made the rounds and distracted the rest of the guests from the near disaster.

"It helps me to think about something else I really want," Barracuda said, to no one in particular. Both Amber and Gavyn hung on every word of his advice. "Sometimes the only thing that can make a craving stop is Carver. Sex, I mean. It's not worth it, Gav. Just think, if you have one, you'll have a dozen. Tomorrow you won't even remember your night with Amber. Don't do that to yourself. Don't delete this happiness from your memory."

Gavyn put his hand on Roman's shoulder as his logic returned. "I'm good now. Thanks. It just...I wasn't expecting it, that's all. It helps when I'm prepared."

"If it gets bad, you come find me." Barracuda slapped Gavyn's back.

"I'm not going to interrupt your fucking wedding night—"

"You will. If you need to, you should. I want you to." He smiled at his new husband. "Carver would say exactly the same thing."

"Okay." Gavyn swallowed hard, some of the cottony feeling dissipating. "Okay, I will. Thank you."

Then he couldn't sit still a moment longer. He shot to his feet and held his hand out to Amber. "Dance with me?"

"I'd love to." She smiled. Except this time her lip wobbled, tempting him to bite the plump flesh she worried between her stark white teeth.

"Don't pity me," he grumbled in her ear as they whirled around the floor in time to the live band, who covered some classic crooner.

"I don't. But I *am* worried about you." Her hand rested high on his back, holding him close to her. "Same as you were for me earlier. Neither one of us has been at our finest today."

"Hey, it's not about perfect, remember?" Though she did a pretty damn terrific imitation of flawless as he held her in his arms and twirled her around.

"Yes. Do you?" She looked up at him, so beautiful and trusting. He could do nothing except earn her respect.

So he nodded and was surprised to feel some of the oily sickness the alcohol debacle had left behind slipping from his soul. They danced and danced, practically fused together, until the food was served, and again after.

Gavyn couldn't believe that Amber left her tablet behind so long and didn't even check to see if the cake cutting happened at the prescribed hour. Things took care of themselves, because she'd done her work in arranging them thoroughly. She went with the flow, enjoyed the moment and lived so fully that she hurt to look at.

Gorgeous and bold, she was unstoppable in his eyes.

When, finally, the guests began to wander away to their own cabins, she made her final rounds with the vendors and her clients. She hugged her sister tight and offered her blessings one more time. Assured that everything was taken care of for the rest of the night, she held out her hand and Gavyn wasted no time in taking it.

"Walk me home, Gavyn?" she asked.

"How about something faster? Can I run you there instead?" He bent down and scooped her into his arms, loving the sound of her riotous laughter. The guests burst into a round of applause as he carried her off into the night, Roman and Nola hooting loudest of all. She tossed them a royal wave at their spectacular exit.

At the edge of the reception area, Gavyn spotted her mother and Tom snuggled together on a bench, looking up at the stars. When Ms. Brown noticed them together, she winked, then went back to her own business.

Gavyn figured that was about the most ringing endorsement he'd ever receive.

Amber tempted him to stop and kiss her senseless with every second that passed. He held off, wanting to seduce her properly this time. Her gown fluttered in the wind as he went as fast as he dared on the slippery path.

Feathers floating on the breeze kept ending up in his mouth, giving him an idea.

"What's that diabolical grin for?" Amber asked as she reached up to free the dress from his lips.

"You'll see," he promised. He couldn't help but reflect her seductive smile as he finally made it to her cabin, which seemed like it had taken forever. He took the stairs two at a time and practically crashed through the door.

CHAPTER EIGHT

G avyn kicked the door shut and marched to the studio-style cabin's bed, which was the fancy four-poster kind with mosquito netting draped from the top. It reminded him of their indiscretion at the pergola the day before, and he hummed.

He set Amber on the mattress gently then followed her down. His shoes hit the floor with a double-clunk as he toed them off before crawling between her legs. He lifted first one then the other, running his hands along her toned calves to her ankles then slipping her high-heels from her feet. Though honestly, they were fucking hot and seeing her naked except for those would have been a treat.

Tonight, however, he wanted something richer than that. Something more romantic, though no less steamy. Maybe the weddings had rubbed off on him. He needed to feel a connection with Amber that went deeper than physical.

It wouldn't be hard.

Placing her feet on the mattress, he smiled as her toes curled in the thick comforter where they peeked from beneath the riot of fluffy feathers. A few had come loose, dangling by a thread here or there. He toyed with one, then plucked it from the dress.

Gavyn set it aside and went to work on getting her naked so they could finally press together, skin on skin, something he'd been craving since before she'd even come to Bare Natural in person. The first time he'd seen her on the videochat screen he'd gotten an insta-hard-on that had hardly let him forget about her since.

Now she was here, smiling up at him, her hair a riot of midnight curls haloing her face. As if he'd made his request out loud, she rolled onto her stomach, leaving the lace-up back of her sinful dress exposed to him. He leaned forward, covering her, dusting her hair out of the way so that he could nibble on the base of her neck.

Amber practically purred. She turned restless, squirming slightly against the bed and his chest. Only then did he lift up enough to untie the sash bow at her waist. With that out of the way, he worked along the crisscrossing back, unwinding the ribbon that had held her tight all day.

She sighed as the pressure released.

Gavyn helped her sit up, amused when she crossed her arms, cupping her breasts as the bodice of her dress tumbled into her lap. She rested in a pool of luxurious purple satin and feathers, looking every bit like a pin-up girl or maybe a classy centerfold.

"Beautiful," he murmured.

Everything he did was slowed by their endless kisses. He couldn't help himself from taking a new taste of her every few seconds, and she seemed as hungry as he was. Amber forgot her modesty long enough to bury her fingers in his hair and knead his scalp as she met him for endless sweeps of their lips over each other's.

When he couldn't stand to wait any longer, he cupped the unharmed side of her face and drew his thumb down her lips, loving how swollen and rouged they were from their exchange. Her eyes were large and bright, even in the dim light, supplied only by the moon and the stars.

Gavyn tucked his fingers in the sides of her dress and shimmied it lower until she had to lift her ass off the bed so he could sweep it from beneath her. He paused briefly to admire the elegant black panties she'd paired with her outfit, a tangle of strings and lace that hardly covered her pussy.

He nuzzled her there, breathing deep as he continued to peel the dress down her thighs then, finally, off her entirely. He flung it to the floor so that he could simply look at her, almost-naked and willing, before him.

Again, he surrendered to the lure of her mouth and returned to kissing her before her soft moans escalated and he couldn't resist the invitation she was making by writhing against his still-clothed body. He traveled down her torso, starting with her neck then licking a line to her breasts. He toyed with them, slowly, gently, in a way he'd never found particularly pleasing before.

With Amber, he didn't want to rush. Didn't want to binge. He wanted to savor.

So he did.

She gasped when he kissed her stomach, licking and softly biting the tight skin around her bellybutton, all the while stroking her arms and long legs and anything else he could reach. In advance of his mouth's arrival, he slipped her panties from her curvaceous form, loving the way her hips fit his palms and would give him a perfect grip when he fucked her from behind.

"Maybe you're right," he said softly, afraid to shatter the moment. "Perfection is looking better from where I'm lying right now."

To him, she was flawless.

Her fingers returned to his hair, entwining in it as she urged him between her legs.

He chuckled before lifting her to remove her underwear completely, then spreading her thighs wide around his torso, giving himself a prime view of her pretty pussy. "I'm getting there, love."

"Quicker," she moaned.

"Is this what you want?" he asked as he dipped forward, plying her glistening folds with his outstretched tongue.

"God yes!" Amber rose up to meet him, her long body arching in response to the barest of contact.

Happy to give them both what they desired, he pressed deeper into her core, sucking lightly on her pussy as he brought his hands to her knees and pushed outward. With better access, he drove forward again, circling her entrance with long laps before spearing his tongue inside her as deeply as he could reach. His nose rubbed her clit as he feasted on her, enjoying the taste of her so much that he almost forgot this was intended to be for her pleasure and not his.

Win-win, he supposed.

Gavyn smiled against her when she reached for his hand, holding it and rubbing her thumb over his knuckles as he continued to eat her greedily. She rained an intermittent string of moans over him, adding to the decadent sensations. Unlike the too-consistent fake cries of some of his fucks, who seemed to think he'd take their silence as an insult, Amber's reactions were honest and organic.

Every time she groaned or hissed or cursed, he redoubled his efforts, intent on making her do it again. When her thighs began to quiver around him, he knew she was holding back on purpose. He scooped his hands beneath her ass and lifted her pelvis to his face, allowing her no room for retreat or half-measures.

"I could do this all night, Amber," he muttered against her body. "Come on my face. I'll take you there again. As many times as you want."

As if his breath washing over her—or maybe his promise—was enough to set her free, she cried out. Loud and desperate. So he returned to his feast, paying special attention to her clit as he manipulated her with his mouth.

Though she didn't seem to need it, he couldn't help but feel her as she surrendered, so he slid one finger inside her clinging sheath and grinned against her when the penetration triggered her orgasm. She clamped around him violently, shuddering and writhing until he laid one arm across her middle, keeping her in place.

And when she seemed wrung dry, he diverted to less sensitive tissue without stopping, taking his time to build her back up as he'd promised. By the third or fourth time she exploded, she started begging.

"Please, Gavyn. Come here. Take off your clothes. I want to see you. Touch you. Ride you," she admitted.

That last one got him. To see her towering over him, glorious and proud as she worked his cock with her body... Well, he was human after all, and resisting what they both wanted would be impossible.

He loosened his tie and yanked it over his head, setting it on the pillow with the almost-forgotten feather before slowly and methodically taking first his suit jacket, then his shirt, off button by button.

Amber touched herself, squeezing her breasts and rubbing her pussy as she watched him strip for her pleasure. "You're so damn handsome. Ripped. I can't wait to feel your muscles flexing as you're fucking me."

"Keep talking like that and it won't be the kind of ride I want to give you, love." He groaned.

She lunged up and snatched at his belt buckle, making him laugh. When was the last time he'd done that in bed?

Still, he picked up the pace, if only a little, divesting himself of his pants, underwear and socks, leaving himself completely nude. Amber's gaze roamed from his pecs to his abs then to his cock, which he was sure had never been so hard in all his life. She licked her lips as she studied him rolling on a condom, then kept going to his thighs before coming back to his erection.

"Can I touch you?" she asked, her hand reaching out anyway.

"You can do anything you want to me." He grinned.

"Really? You should be careful. There are some things I've never had the guts to try with a guy." The downright naughty smile she tossed him had him groaning. He'd submit to anything if it brought her bliss.

"Later," he said. "After we've done this a few dozen times and I can think straight again. Feel free to experiment as much as you like."

"I will." She lifted her arms, welcoming him back.

They both moaned when their bodies aligned for the first time with nothing between them. His cock nudged at her thigh and she wriggled, trying to fit herself to it. When Gavyn resisted, content to hold her and kiss her for a while longer, she protested.

Amber rolled them so that he was lying on his back with her straddling his hips. She reached down between them and pumped his cock in her supple palm a few times.

As if he wasn't already stiffer than the curtain rods they'd installed the day before.

He watched her, though, because the image of her darker skin against his, cradling him, was alluring and intimate. And when she lifted up a fraction of an inch, angling his cock toward her pussy, he thought he would die from the excitement of witnessing himself enter her. Bit by bit.

Clenching rings of muscle gave way, slowly yielding to gravity and the pressure of his rounded head. It nearly made his head explode as her body stroked his dick from the tip then onto the shaft.

Amber lifted herself then returned, bearing down on him until he was fully embedded in her heat. They stayed locked like that, unmoving, for a long time. First staring into each other's eyes, then kissing when he reached for her and drew her onto his chest.

He'd never had sex like this before. Made love, he supposed. It'd never been so slow and achingly tender. Never something he was afraid of.

Scared because he knew that it would never satisfy him again to have a quick and meaningless fuck after he'd experienced something so utterly mind-blowing.

Eventually, their make out session turned into fucking as Amber slowly rocked her hips while she grazed her mouth across his lips, chin and neck. She ground on him, clenching him tight within her as she worked over him in a sinuous figure eight that rubbed her clit against the pad of muscle at the base of his cock.

He smiled up at her as she began to rock faster, moan louder and draw tighter around him.

"That's it, love," he coached her. "Come on me."

"Want to wait for you," she whimpered.

"Not this time." He still had plenty to give her. "Keep taking, as much as you can."

Amber's eyes grew wide, looking nearly molten in the moonlight. She let him guide her hips, helping her maintain her rhythm as her conscious thoughts were likely overwhelmed by desire. When she bucked, causing him to bore inside her as deeply as possible, then went stiff in his hold and screamed his name, he prayed he could keep his word.

It had never been so difficult to stave off his orgasm as when she unraveled around him.

Then again, he hadn't done this much without a good helping of whiskey dick either.

It wasn't that—he knew it wasn't—that lured him toward climax.

It was all her.

He wanted to experience that lust again. And again.

That thought alone saved him.

Gavyn gathered her to him and rolled, bringing them to their sides so he could croon praise and reassurance to her as she continued to crest for so long he couldn't tell if she had come down and starting orgasming again or if she was just this incredibly responsive.

Either way, he petted her. Her back, her shoulders, her arms, her thighs, her breasts. He sucked on her nipples, while still embedded in her fully.

When her sighs turned back to soft moans, he began to thrust.

Gavyn drew one of her knees up so that it draped over his hip and shuttled within her. He withdrew until only the barest bit of him remained inside her, then flexed until he had buried himself as deep as possible.

After his arm had long gone numb and they'd kissed each other's lips raw, he pressed her to the bed, riding her faster and with shorter strokes.

It didn't take more than a few minutes before she shattered while staring up at him with dreamy, blissed-out eyes. She needed a break, or she'd be completely overwhelmed. Frankly, so did his cock, which was dying for release.

So he pulled out of her, making both of them groan at the loss.

Instead of jacking off on her tits or whatever else it was she seemed to expect, he reached for the supplies he'd left at the head of the bed earlier.

He ordered, "Turn over."

She obeyed without hesitation.

"Good girl." He squeezed her ass hard before landing a spank there that made her yelp. Still she didn't pull away. "Tell me if you're not into this."

"I am, Gav. I am." She sighed and spread her legs as if she missed his cock in her pussy as much as he did.

Without waiting for her to change her mind, he tugged her hands into the small of her back, stacked her wrists on top of one another, then bound them with the silk he'd worn all day. She tugged against the knot, but didn't get anywhere.

"Still good?"

"So good," she whispered.

"That's right, love," he murmured to her as he held himself over her with one arm while kissing and rubbing every inch of skin on her backside. He followed the moist heat of his tongue with a swipe of the cool feather, making her tremble and moan.

At some point, he lifted her ass, bringing her to her knees with her shoulders planted on the bed. He rotated her face so that her fractured cheek was up, in no danger of him injuring it further, before proceeding. When Amber realized what he was doing, she smiled at him and murmured, "Thank you."

He kissed her yet again before trailing the feather over her lips then along her neck to her graceful back. He toyed with her for as long as they both could stand. Stroking his cock idly, he tickled the bottom of her foot. She jerked and cried out.

"Is there a problem?" He knew there wasn't. Except that she was growing needy again.

"I'm so turned on," Amber confessed. "Every tiny touch feels so strong. My whole body is alive, aching for you."

Gavyn rewarded her by cupping her mound in his palm.

She shouted his name and rubbed herself on him. He had a front row seat to the flexing of her pussy, which was slathered with her arousal. He made one last circuit with the feather, this time around her asshole, and when she clenched instinctively, he worked his thumb into her cunt, giving her something to hold.

"Oh God. You're driving me crazy." She pleaded with him, "Fuck me, Gavyn. Please. Fuck me again. Harder this time. Please."

Who was he to say no?

He leaned forward only long enough to lap at her pussy a few times, tasting the proof of her rapture. Then he gripped his cock in one hand, the tie binding her hands in the other, and penetrated her with a single thrust that landed him balls-deep in her pussy.

"Oh fuck. Amber." He groaned, not unaffected himself. "You *are* perfect. This. Is. perfect."

He did as she asked and as his body demanded, finally riding her hard and fast. Her ass slapped against his abs and she chanted his name, encouraging him to fuck. So he did. And when she exploded, he nearly went with her.

Biting the inside of his cheek, he found a well of self-control he hadn't known he possessed. Didn't before her.

He withdrew and tended to Amber, untying her hands and ensuring the circulation hadn't been cut off, rubbing her wrists as she gasped for air and reveled in her ongoing climax.

She opened one eye and looked up at him. "You still didn't come?"

"I'm about to." He grinned. "If you've got one more in you."

"I..." She sighed. "I'm good. Use me to get yourself off. God, Gavyn. You're the best lover I've ever had. Please, just do whatever makes you feel best."

He smiled and rubbed his nose lightly along hers. "If you insist."

"I do." Amber inhaled sharply when he reintroduced his cock to her pussy. She hugged him tight—with her arms clutching his neck, her legs wrapped around his waist, and her cunt sucking at him relentlessly.

"But you're coming with me," he told her.

"I can't," she protested.

"You will." He guaranteed it.

Gavyn didn't have any fancy tricks to ensure she would. Their chemistry and the connection they had built did all the work for him. She responded as he loosened his hold on himself, reacting to each of his honest emotions with some of her own.

He pumped inside her with long, languid strokes that felt more like gliding than thrusting. The ring of muscles at her entrance strangled him, preventing him from falling from her body as he pistoned within her. And when the sweet silk of her pussy began to undulate around him, he knew they both were goners.

He kissed her one last time, staring directly into her eyes as he let ecstasy consume him. It started at the base of his cock and worked outward, a rapture so divine, he swore they'd reached heaven together.

"Go ahead, Gavyn." Amber sealed his fate. "I want to feel your cock jerking in my pussy with every pump. Watch me come with you and know that no one has ever fucked me so well. You're perfect for me, Gavyn."

It'd been so long since he felt like he was worth anything, her words touched the deepest parts of him. There was no option except to do as she asked. Especially when she screamed and climaxed around him once more.

He came with a roar, plunging to the very limits of her pussy before unleashing stream after stream of semen. There had never been an orgasm in the history of man as strong or satisfying as that one, he was pretty sure.

Gavyn kept coming, fucking gently into Amber as she hugged him tight and her cunt milked him with her answering climax. It went on for hours, or at least it seemed like it, until they both collapsed into a sweaty, worn-out tangle of limbs.

Afraid of crushing her, he flopped to his back and drew Amber to him until she draped over his chest. They lay that way for a while, stunned, with her listening to his racing heart as it eventually settled into its regular beat.

"What happens now?" he asked, immediately regretting it. Well, Tom *had* told him to be vulnerable.

"I hope you'll stay. Maybe we can sleep for a while?" She sounded hopeful and exhausted simultaneously.

He could have let it go, except suddenly it mattered. A lot. "I meant when you go home."

"Oh." She shrugged. "You're the expert with this kind of thing. Mr. Spontaneity. I assumed we'd do our best to wring the most enjoyment out of these next couple days then go our separate ways and think of each other fondly. That's what you do...right?"

It was.

Until her.

Was that what she wanted, or what she expected? They were two totally different things. Or maybe he was overreaching. Sure, he was a good fuck, but he'd be a shitty excuse for a boyfriend or husband, never knowing when he might crack again.

"Gavyn?" Amber must have sensed the tension coiling his muscles, sabotaging the relief she'd granted him, without even trying.

"Shhh." He stroked her hair. "Ignore me. I shouldn't have mentioned it."

She seemed like she might press the issue at first. After a minute she relaxed, then whispered, "Okay."

Was it his imagination, or did she sound disappointed?

In him, or *with* him?

Neither would be great and the stakes had just gotten raised so much higher. He'd never imagined he could find someone so perfectly suited for him in and out of bed.

Gavyn kept caressing her, trying to memorize the satiny feel of her skin. Before long, her breathing evened out and she surrendered to the utter fatigue plaguing her. He continued to hold her for as long as he could before the misery of his impending loss of her spiraled him into a black depression, stealing his ability to sleep.

Carefully, he untangled himself from her and slipped out of bed.

CHAPTER NINE

For a long time Gavyn stood there, watching Amber sleep. What they'd shared was epic...and disastrous. At least for him. Because now he was sure that he'd never in all his life have something as brilliant as her.

He'd ruined himself before he even had a chance.

A woman who prized perfection and stability could never settle for someone as irreparably broken as him for a life partner.

Inherently flawed.

Incurably sick.

He paced the cabin. On the path leading farther away from the bed, he thought up every reason he was horrible for her, admitting he should leave her alone before he fucked up her life. On the way back, when he could see her lying there, so heartbreakingly beautiful, he argued with himself about how he'd do better for her. Over and over, he resolved to wake her up and tell her he wanted to try for something that went beyond a wedding affair.

Yet every time he approached her, he chickened out. So he'd nearly worn a groove in the plank flooring by the time his restless energy was depleted.

Though he was exhausted, physically and mentally drained, he couldn't bring himself to return to the bed where they'd shared the most amazing experience of his life, because he didn't want to taint her with his presence. He thought about bailing, crossing the lawn to his cabin and pretending like the one-night stand had been nothing extraordinary. With his hand on the doorknob, he couldn't force his wrist to turn. Torn, he headed instead for the same couch on which he'd spent the predawn hours the morning before.

He plopped down, unconcerned about his nudity, and flung himself onto his side with enough drama to suit a thirteen-year-old girl who hadn't gotten asked to the spring dance.

That was when he saw the gift someone had so thoughtfully snuck into Amber's cottage.

A black ice bucket with the distinct gleaming gold foil of a bottle of Cristal peeking out from the top.

Gavyn rocketed to a sitting position. His spine whipped so straight, so fast, it nearly cracked. He lunged for the champagne and cradled the bottle to his chest as if it were a precious baby instead of a hell of a good vintage.

The folded note looped around the neck read, *I hope you don't mind this one surprise addition to your agenda. Thank you for everything. I love you. Enjoy, Nola.*

Gavyn had the neck of the bottle exposed quicker than he'd unwrapped Amber from her dress earlier. Before he even knew what he was doing, he'd popped the cork, sending it flying across the room.

Foam gushed from the bottle, covering his hands with sweet-smelling alcohol. Not letting it go to waste, he licked it up greedily, not missing a drop from his palms.

Then he froze. He stared in horror at his glimmering hands as if they were coated in blood after a brutal murder. Then he glanced over his shoulder at Amber, who'd slept through the noise. She was dead to the world.

To his transgression.

He couldn't control himself. He couldn't stop.

He wanted to, for her sake. This wasn't the kind of man she deserved to be stuck with. Was it?

Desperate, he plunked the champagne on the coffee table, pried his fingers from the lovely bottle one at a time then slid onto the floor and crawled to his discarded clothes. He hauled his phone from his suit pants.

Gavyn made his way to the bathroom and locked himself in so Amber wouldn't hear or be woken by the glow from his phone. Also so he wouldn't run over to the champagne and chug the entire bottle before someone could stop him.

He needed help. Eyes scrunched closed, unable to believe he was going to interrupt Barracuda's wedding night for something so pitiful, he considered his options.

It was either that or wake Amber and admit how fucked up he really was, guaranteeing he'd have no chance with her in any case.

Sweating and shaking, he could barely thumb through his contacts in search of Roman's name. The fingers of his other hand clenched and unclenched as he tried to ignore the voices screaming at him to forget this and go into the other room instead.

Just then he pulled up Barracuda's number. When he finally got it on screen, he jabbed the icon before he could change his mind. Again.

It rang. And rang and rang.

Roman didn't answer.

"Fuck!" He punched the wall by the sink hard enough to skin his knuckles, dropping his phone in the process. It shattered on the tile floor, severing his only lifeline.

It was hopeless. *He* was hopeless.

Why had Roman been able to fix himself when Gavyn couldn't?

Overwhelmed, he surrendered.

He opened the bathroom door and took a step toward the bottle taunting him. He sniffed his own hands, just for a fix. One taste, that was all—he needed one taste and then he would go search out his friend.

Except the instant his hand wrapped around the bottle's neck, he knew there was no stopping now.

Gavyn tipped it to his lips and drank.

And drank.

And drank some more.

It burned as it fizzled down his throat.

He welcomed the pain.

Gasping for air, he realized he'd slammed half the bottle in one pull and prepared to finish it, get it over with, with the next. When it was empty, some dribbling onto his chest from where it had overflowed his mouth, he dropped the bottle onto the couch.

Gavyn grabbed the pen and the note from Nola and scrawled on the back of it. He staggered over to the bed and placed the paper beside Amber. Though he wished he could lean forward and kiss her one more time, he refused to defile her like that.

Instead, he slunk to the door and escaped before she could cage him in, away from what he needed. Not that she would care about him anymore if she saw what he had done. Who he really was. All that talk of changing was bullshit.

She was right to play by the rules. They kept her safe.

From herself.

And from the disappointing elements of the world. Including him.

He tried to run when his feet hit the ground, not caring that sticks and rocks and wet dirt clung to his soles. The champagne hit him hard, going to his head and making him dizzy.

Gavyn crashed, face first into the dirt, only laughing raucously when a rock smashed into his ribs. He deserved for it to hurt. It'd been so long since he'd had a drink, he could hardly hold his liquor anymore. What a pussy.

He'd fix that. The catering supplies wouldn't be hauled away for a solid three or four hours yet, according to Amber's schedule. He'd make the most of that open bar after all.

CHAPTER TEN

A sharp knock on the door startled Amber. Fast asleep, she struggled to surface from the coma she'd fallen into after making love with Gavyn.

"Gav?" she called sleepily. "Is that you?"

Maybe he'd gotten locked out after using Kayla and Dave's kitchen to cook them another spectacular breakfast. One she would eagerly devour. Sex with him was better than cardio for working up her appetite.

"No, sorry. It's me. Roman." His voice came quietly from the front of the cabin as if he was unsure or trying not to frighten her. "The door's not shut all the way—mind if I come in?"

What the hell?

"Yes! I mean...I mind. Hang on a minute." Amber scrambled to engage her brain. She lunged for a blanket to wrap around her nude body, snatched the gold condom wrapper off the sheets, sprang out of bed and promptly tripped over one of Gavyn's dress shoes.

Where is he?

Her body reminded her, with delicious aches, of the time they'd spent together the night before, making love in a variety of poses she didn't usually subject herself to. Maybe Sabra had something with that yoga stuff. If Amber was going to be getting it on with a super-stud more often, she'd have to get into better shape. Be more flexible. In all sorts of ways.

Holy hell. He'd practically knocked her unconscious. She hadn't slept like that since she was a child, with nothing to worry about. Since before her father had died.

Swiping the tangle of her hair from her face, she tried to appear a tiny bit together. No hope, really.

Barracuda grinned at her when she approached. "If I wasn't a happily married man, I'd have to say... Damn, Amber."

She blushed despite her newly turned wild leaf.

"Sorry. I was...really tired. Are you waiting for Gavyn? Is he in the shower?" She peeked toward the bathroom. The door was wide open and there was something on the floor.

"Actually, I was coming to see if everything was okay." Roman snapped back to serious awfully quick. "I didn't realize my phone had run out of battery last night. When I plugged it in this morning I saw I had a 2am missed call from him."

"What?" A sick feeling swirled around her stomach. "You did?"

"Yeah." His gaze began to dart around the room uneasily. For a badass like Roman, that was about as concerning as full-blown hysterics from a regular human being.

Right about then, she realized the object now crumpled in her hand was paper, not plastic, and the condom wrapper had been black, not gold.

"Oh shit." Amber unfurled her fingers and realized it was actually a note. From her sister? And on the back... Two words scrawled in a barely legible script.

I'm sorry.

"No!" she cried out at the same time Roman started cursing violently, inventing new combinations she'd never heard before. He grabbed something off the couch and held it up to her.

"Please tell me you drank this." Barracuda waved a fancy champagne bottle.

Amber put her face in her hands, her cheek objecting though nothing could hurt as much as her cracking heart. Her knees gave out and she fell to them on the floor, sobbing. "I didn't know it was there. I swear I didn't."

"It's not your fault." Roman rushed to her side. His phone was already halfway to his ear. And seconds later, he was barking out orders. "Meep. I need you. And the rest of the guys. Gavyn is missing. I think he's on a bender. Run down to the lot and make sure his motorcycle is still here. If it is, then help me search the grounds. We've got to find him. Quick."

As if he'd urged Amber on instead of his new husband, Roman's instructions clicked in her mind. She didn't give a shit if he saw her naked. She ditched the blanket and drew on Gavyn's shirt, which covered her almost to her knees. Good enough.

"Let's go." She grabbed Roman's hand, tugging him toward the door, as he stood still gaping at her.

"Amber, I know you don't want to hear this right now, but...I think you should stay," he tried to warn her. "No matter what we find, it's not going to be pretty and—"

"I'm not going to leave him out there alone. He could be hurt. In trouble..." Her voice cracked. "Worse."

"Think positive." Barracuda hugged her then conceded, probably because arguing about it was wasting too much time.

She didn't even bother to put on shoes before they darted out of the cabin.

Roman immediately began searching the area around the cute bungalow while she sprinted over to the one Gavyn had been staying in. The door smashed against the wall with a bang. It was pretty clear he hadn't been there since he'd retrieved his suit the day before. The bed was neatly made. Everything was in order.

Still, she checked the bathroom and the floor before giving up hope that he'd come over here to sleep off the champagne. They hadn't gotten lucky enough for him to quit with that one bottle. She could attest to his tenacity. If he drank like he fucked, then this was going to be bad.

Really bad.

Amber muffled a sob then dashed back outside, nearly colliding with Roman.

"He's not in here," she reported.

"Not anywhere outside either."

They looked at each other, exchanging panic. Her eyes closed and she thought of all the places he could have gone. Just then, Barracuda's phone rang.

He answered, putting it on speaker. "What do you have, Meep?"

"Good news. All the vehicles are accounted for, including Gavyn's chopper," Carver told them. "He's still here. Somewhere."

141

Amber's worry eased a tiny bit as she erased images of him splattered across the pavement from the horrific reel of movies running through her imagination. "Thank God."

"Got it. Thanks. Can you get the rest of the gang, and the crew too, to help search?" Roman asked.

"On it," he confirmed. Then, just before he hung up, he said, "I love you, Roman. Tell Amber I love her too."

Roman looked at the disconnected phone in his hand and then to her. He assured her, "We'll find him."

How cold had it gotten the night before? The rain had brought some cooler air behind it. Though they were on the downhill slide to summer, she was shivering after only a few minutes of exposure. Or maybe that was sheer terror causing her to tremble.

Where would he have likely gone?

"Oh no." She looked up and found Roman staring back at her as if he'd had the same idea simultaneously.

"The bar. Everything is still in the pavilion, isn't it?" He grimaced.

"My fault. It's my damn fault. I knew it was a problem for him and I didn't have it taken away." She couldn't help the tears that fell from her eyes. How could she have been so lax that she didn't protect the one person who'd needed her lately?

"I told you, this is *not* your responsibility." Roman frightened her a little with the ferocity of his snarl. "Look, I hurt Carver with my bullshit too. And I guarantee that's the last thing Gavyn would want for you right now. He owns this. Me too, for not answering the motherfucking phone after I said I would. But we have to put that aside for now. Let's find him first. There will be plenty of time for playing *what if* later."

Amber nodded. She still couldn't help the guilt eating her alive. They both knew there would be so many nights filled with regret that none of them would escape unscathed.

Except Roman hadn't seen the sides of Gavyn she had. He was generous, funny, smart and kind, when life allowed him to be. Anything she'd done to obstruct his progress would haunt her for the rest of her days.

Worse, if he had—

She couldn't bring herself to think of what might have happened to him.

Instead, she jumped off the porch and sprinted for the wedding pavilion. Although Roman had been flat-footed, he caught up quickly then surpassed her pace. Probably he didn't want her stumbling over Gavyn's corpse if he'd choked to death on his own vomit.

The thought nearly made her blackout.

Amber tripped. Gravel skinned her knees. She picked herself up and kept going despite the warm trickles of blood she could feel running down her shins.

Pumping her arms, she ran faster.

Roman shouted, "Son of a bitch!" By his tone, she could tell he hadn't found what he was looking for. Was that a good sign or a bad one?

Barreling into the pavilion, she was shocked at the mess.

Empty bottles littered the bar. Several of them were broken, along with a slew of glasses and the mirror showcasing the liquor, as if Gavyn had raged as he poisoned himself.

Amber swallowed hard. Why had this happened?

She'd gone to sleep steeped in euphoria. Hadn't he?

What had caused him to be so angry? What had she done wrong?

"Gavyn?" Roman bellowed as he hunted around, flipping the tables to search beneath them while she rummaged through the shrubs nearby.

Something in Amber's gut told her he hadn't stuck around after he'd gotten his fill.

Think! she screamed at herself, though it was practically impossible given the galloping of her heart, the unanswered questions barraging her mind and the adrenaline-fueled horror pegging her vitals at the moment.

Where would he go?

She looked at the smashed bar and scoured her mind for anything that might bring him comfort.

"I know his favorite place at the resort. The hammock over the koi pond." Amber took off, not waiting for Roman, who could easily catch up given his longer stride and the boots he'd been sensible enough to tug on before coming to check up on Gavyn.

She skipped the less direct paved paths, not caring about the branches that slapped her exposed legs or even the one that smacked her cheek, causing her to shriek.

"Amber, hang on!" Roman shouted to her, but she didn't listen. "Slow down!"

Unlike the methodical approach she'd have taken in any other situation, she trusted her instincts and flew. Cutting through the flower gardens might have been a mistake, given the number of rose bushes and the thorns that shredded Gavyn's shirt. Still, the minor pains had nothing on her mounting terror.

After drinking everything they'd seen empty at the bar, he was in serious trouble. At least, she hoped he was still in danger and not beyond assistance.

She smashed through the last of the greenery separating her from the spot she'd first truly made out with Gavyn, and nearly toppled into the pond.

He was there.

Facedown.

Unmoving.

Buck-naked.

His skin bearing an unnatural blue tint.

"No!" Amber screamed. The sound seemed to come from far away in her mind, as if it had been made by a mortally wounded animal somewhere on the mountainside.

"Amber!" Roman shouted from close behind as he joined her. "Oh no. No. Gavyn! Fuck, no."

"Shut up." Gavyn groaned, clutched his head then puked into the pond.

He wasn't dead.

Oh God. Amber's heart nearly pounded out of her chest. Her feet were glued to the grass. About that time, Carver charged into the area, clued in to their location by their shrieks, no doubt.

"Help me get him," Roman begged Carver. Meep didn't need to be asked. He'd already

146

climbed onto the knotted rope, making it rock.

Which only made Gavyn more ill.

Amber hoped that was a good thing, clearing some of the alcohol from his system. Still she couldn't make herself budge.

When Roman clamped his hand around Gavyn's ankle, he hissed. "He's freezing."

Together, the two men hauled Gavyn to solid ground, then Meep stripped off his shirt and attempted to get it over Gavyn's head. Impossible with him fighting them every step of the way.

"Gavyn, let them help you," she pleaded, hating the hoarse tremble of her voice.

He slumped in Roman and Carver's arms, then lifted his head far enough to look at her. Only for a second.

"Get her th' fuck 'way from me!" Gavyn bellow-slurred before wrenching free of the pair of Hot Rods. He crashed to his hands and knees and got sick again.

She didn't know what she'd done to repulse him so much. To drive him to this after their night together.

Confused and afraid of making the situation worse, Amber turned to Roman. Tears streamed down her cheeks as she asked him, "Will you take care of him for me?"

"Of course," he answered. He leaned toward her, as if he wanted to hug her, but his hands were decidedly full of pissed off, drunk, alcohol-poisoned man. "Have someone call an ambulance. We're going to need to take him for treatment and he's not going to go willingly."

"Fuck! No!" Gavyn raged against the pair of guys whose support had turned to restraint.

"I already called 911," Meep told them. "Help is coming. Dave is out front, waiting for them to arrive."

"Fuck you!" Gavyn took a swing at Carver that the sober man easily dodged. "Let me die already, would you?"

"No can do, friend."

"If you harm one hair on Meep—accident or not—I *will* knock you out and make this easier on us all," Barracuda snarled. "It's bad enough you've hurt Amber. Quit fighting and let us help you."

"Amber?" For a moment Gavyn went limp in their grip, nearly smashing onto the ground again. "Sorry."

"Me too," she whispered, though she couldn't say what for.

"Go ahead, honey," Carver encouraged her, distracting her from Gavyn's mournful gaze. She glanced over to see Meep watching her, his eyes full of empathy that nearly broke her. When she turned back to Gavyn, he would no longer look at her.

So she did as they each had requested.

She turned and walked away.

From the man who'd taught her to break the rules and who was too damn good at that himself. She left part of her heart bleeding there on the grass beside him, afraid he'd never realize what he could have had, if only he'd stayed to claim it.

When she made it around a curve in the path, she buckled. She dropped to the ground and sobbed, thinking she should tell the rest of the Hot Rods and Powertools that they'd found Gavyn and where to go when help arrived, but unable to move. It didn't matter, though. Within seconds, footsteps pounded on the path as someone flew toward her.

Amber tried to stand or simply scoot out of the way. She couldn't make her shocked muscles respond in time. Luckily, Tom was in awesome shape. When he would have plowed into her, he leapt, hurdling her instead before racing back to make sure she was okay.

As if.

"Willie!" he shouted. "I've got Amber."

She'd never been so happy to see her mother in all her life as when the woman trotted into sight. "Amber! Amber, what happened?"

"I don't know." Dazed, destroyed, she kept asking herself the same damn thing.

"Did you two have a fight or something?" her mom asked.

"No." She sniffled. "No. It was nothing like that. We...were together. It was amazing. I fell asleep. And when I woke up, he was gone."

Amber glanced up at the concerned friends beginning to stream past. Some stayed, hovering around her, while others went to guide the paramedics to their location, and still more—the guys, mostly—continued on to help Roman and Carver contain Gavyn.

Nola joined them next, her eyes bloodshot and puffy. "It was the champagne I left for you, wasn't it? I'm so sorry, Amber. I didn't think. Even when you left with him, I thought of you guys going to his cabin not yours. I was so happy and there were so many things happening. I should have warned—"

Amber shushed her sister. At the end of the day, Gavyn had to be responsible for himself. She knew that, despite the fact that she kept trying to imagine what she could have done differently herself.

She wiped her nose on the sleeve of his shirt. No one commented about how she was wearing only that, ruined now from the grime, snot and blood smeared over it.

Her mother wrapped her in her arms and rocked her, promising things would be okay, even though they both knew that was a big, fat lie. Tom approached from her other side, adding his support. Nola completed the circle, hugging her tight even as she cried silently, her tears soaking the neck of Gavyn's shirt.

"You know, I'd kick that boy's ass if he hadn't done so much harm to himself already." Her mom snapped as she stroked Amber's hair.

After several minutes, when her shaking had subsided to minor trembles, Tom and her mom each put one of her arms around their shoulders and stood, bracketing her as the three of them walked the rest of the way to Kayla and Dave's house together. Inside, warmth, compassion, family and friends waited to nurse her superficial wounds.

There was nothing they could do to mend her broken heart.

Not even the news, hours later, that Gavyn was physically in the clear could do that.

CHAPTER ELEVEN

Three Months Later

Gavyn sat in the parking lot of Middletown's hospital, debating whether or not he should get off his motorcycle or turn around and trek the long hours back to Bare Natural. The Powertools crew had asked him to go on their behalf, to congratulate the Hot Rods and welcome their littlest member into the world, but he couldn't decide if they truly appreciated his flexibility—AKA the fact that he still had no job—or if they were making excuses to send him across state lines as part of some misguided matchmaking scheme.

Was this the right thing to do?

He'd spent a lot of time asking himself that lately. Learning to trust himself had been one of the hardest things he'd done since his grand breakdown the night of the Hot Rods' wedding.

The night he'd destroyed his future. Again. Well, one he *might* have had. He'd begun to salvage the wreckage of his life, determined to rebuild it the best he could. Only fitting since he still planned to open his own bike shop. Actually...that was the other reason he'd come.

For help.

He'd started thinking of himself as a project. Knock off some rust here, put in replacement parts there, and soon he'd be roadworthy again. Well, he thought he might be to that point already. Now it was time to focus on professional matters.

Opening his shop by the end of the year had become an official goal.

Except sitting here, looking at a building he knew Amber Brown had recently stood inside was enough to make his chest ache. Would seeing her friends help or hurt his progress?

Maybe if she'd answered his long, detailed apology email—not with forgiveness, he didn't expect that, but with any sort of acknowledgement—he might not feel so out of place.

Still, he knew he owed the Hot Rods an in-person visit. After all, several of them had been responsible for saving his life, giving him a chance to start new—if not as innocently as the baby Kaige and Nola had created and would raise together with their friends.

It was the decent thing to do. He had resolved he would stick to that path, even when it wasn't easy, from now on. So far, so good.

Just to be extra careful, because he'd learned to moderate his reckless behavior some, he took out his phone and texted Roman.

I'm here. Amber's gone, right?

He sat there, swallowing hard, his hands fidgeting with the touch screen until the cell buzzed in his palm.

Yes. But I still think it would be better if she wasn't. I can call her back.

No "but", Roman. I won't do that to her. If she wants to talk to me ever again, she knows where to find me.

Okay, well, maybe not at the moment she didn't. But she could easily find out. Yet hadn't.

Relieved, Gavyn climbed from the bike and snagged the package Kayla had given him before he left early that morning. Along with a lecture only a sibling could deliver, like the closing arguments of a high-profile case, about what she thought was best for him. Oddly, her version had sounded a lot like what Roman argued as well.

Damn them for putting rogue ideas in his brain. It was better to forget and move on.

No. Strike that. To *go* on. He'd never forget. Not even the preposterous amount of alcohol he'd chugged that night had been able to erase the memory of sleeping with Amber from his warped mind, thank God.

Every night his dreams were filled with her in that gorgeous dress, and then out of it. The way she'd let him have control and enjoyed the hell out of it. Of her snuggled to his chest, sleeping in his arms.

Leaving that bed had easily been the stupidest decision he'd made in his life.

It wasn't easy, but he battled the regret swamping him. Thanks to Amber, actually. The story she'd shared about her mom and her reaction to Mr. Brown's death so many years ago had stuck with him too. If he was to do better for himself, he had to let that go.

Let *her* go.

As much as it hurt.

Because anything else would kill him.

Almost had.

Gavyn shook his head, concentrated on the good around him, including the adorable owls smiling up at him from the colorful package in his hands. The curly mass of ribbons on top reminded him of the rainbow at the Hot Rods' wedding, probably on purpose. And he could smile at that memory.

So he did.

By the time he'd reached the maternity ward, he was in a better frame of mind. He paused at the plate-glass window on the nursery and put his hand on the pane, staring at the tiny babies inside. So much potential.

"Don't waste it, tikes," he said.

Then continued to the room number Roman had texted him.

Laughter and delighted coos echoed from it. He would have knocked on the door but someone, Bryce, was in the way. The place was packed with Hot Rods, practically spilling into the hallway to the chagrin of the passing nurses.

"Hey, how's it going?" Rebel turned and grinned, putting out his hand as soon as he caught sight of Gavyn. The guy had a reputation for being polite and his manners certainly showed through now whether he liked it or not. "Come in."

"Thanks." Gavyn felt awkward with the warm greeting. He clasped Bryce's hand on pure instinct alone. He wasn't sure what to say, but he knew he had to say something as the people in the room parted, making a spot for him in their center.

"Hi, everyone," he started, lamely.

A round of hellos, greetings and slaps on the back from the guys and hugs from the women nearby overwhelmed him with their positivity.

"Before we get to the fun stuff, I just wanted to say thank you to you all for helping me out when I hit rock bottom. Also that I'm sorry for fucking up your honeymoon." He gulped thinking of how imperfect he'd made Amber's event. Then he looked to Nola, who rested in the hospital bed. "And especially for hurting your sister."

"That's enough." Eli, the shop owner, stopped him before he could grovel like he'd intended.

"It's really not." He shrugged. "I appreciate you being kind, though. I hope you know that if there's anything I can ever do for you guys, you only have to ask."

Quinn, who'd been hiding in the corner, piped up, "Will you teach me to ride a motorcycle? Alanso says I have to wait until I get my permit next year."

As easy as that, Gavyn was laughing.

"Well, I wouldn't dare cross Al. He can kick my ass." He blocked the bald man's mock-punch, loving that they weren't treating him like a busted ride held together with duct tape. "What if I take you out on the back of my chopper as much you want while I'm in town? Then when you're old enough, I'll give you lessons on a real bike, not that crotch rocket your fellow Hot Rod prefers."

That was good enough for the kid it seemed. He smiled then went back to playing video games on his portable console. "Sweet!"

"How long you staying?" Roman asked.

"I'm not sure yet." He swallowed, then took a deep breath. "I was thinking about renting a room in that long-term motel over on 33. Kind of scoping out the area for shop locations. Maybe asking you guys to look at my plans some? Tell me if you think this is stupid or if it would interfere with what you've got going on, but I was thinking...maybe...it would be smart to open my place nearby since you've already put Middletown on the map for restorations."

"That's a great idea," Nola said. Her opinion had scared him the most. He wouldn't blame her if she hated him for disrespecting her sister. "We're already adding on a merch room at the garage because of all the people who've been stopping in since the TV show got popular."

Sabra smiled and nodded. "I could even slip in a few crossover segments on *Hot Rods* to get people interested."

"Maybe you could do something with the name to affiliate the shops?" Bryce suggested.

"Hot Rides?" Eli added on to his friend's thought.

Several of them smiled and nodded at that.

"I'd love to spend some time working on bikes." Alanso added, surpassing Gavyn's wildest hopes. "If you'll have me, anyway. I could help out for fun—and bring the kid to learn some new stuff—until you're drawing in enough business to hire a staff and don't need us anymore."

"Wow. That's…" He couldn't believe their generosity. "I can pay you."

"Don't piss us off," Holden grumbled. "We're glad to see you going forward."

"Yeah, well, I learned the hard way that fear of failure only guarantees it's gonna happen anyway." He shook his head.

"That's not an easy lesson." Kaelyn reached out and rubbed his back. "We're proud of you, Gavyn."

He tried to look away, so he could blink his eyes against the burning in them, except there was no space to shift his gaze that another friend didn't occupy. Not a bad problem to have.

"Thank you. Seriously." He cleared his throat. "That's not why I came, I hope you know." Gavyn held the pretty package from the Powertools out to Nola. "This is. Congratulations."

"I appreciate that." She took the present, sitting up far enough that she could grab his hand too. Nola didn't let go for a hell of a lot longer than necessary to transfer his cargo.

He squeezed her fingers lightly in return, hoping she really did understand how damn sorry he was. "Can I see your daughter?"

It wasn't a formality. He genuinely wondered and wouldn't be offended if they said no.

"If you leave here without holding her, I'll be pissed." Kaige said from where he was sitting by the window, rocking slowly, with a pink bundle nestled on his shoulder. A tiny thing.

Could there really be a miniature person in those blankets?

Suddenly he was nervous. "Ah, I've never done that before."

"Neither had most of us," Carver told him. "He'll show you how to do it right. It's worth it."

"Um, okay." Gavyn wasn't sure he should be trusted with something so delicate and precious. But they were all looking at him, expecting him to man up, so he shuffled closer.

Super Nova stood, a giant smile making him look smug and content.

"Gavyn, I'd like you to meet Ambrose Wilhemina Davis." He held out the baby, who squirmed a little then settled down, now magically snugged in the crook of Gavyn's arm. "She's named after my mom, Nola's mom, and...well, Amber—her godmother."

At his elbow, Sally adjusted his position slightly until the baby rested snugly in his arm. It surprised the hell out of him how easy and natural it felt to hold Ambrose.

"Just make sure you've got her neck supported and you're great like that," Mustang reassured him.

The infant weighed nothing. Her miniature fingers curled into the tiniest fist on Earth. However, the punch she delivered to his gut was mighty.

"It's a great name," he said, though he couldn't take his eyes off the child long enough to meet Kaige's stare. An incredible tribute and a fantastic role model too, he thought.

"Well, at least it's not as weird as Amber Brown," Kaige teased. "I'm still not sure what Willie was thinking with that one. Double colors? Brownish McBrownster?"

"Why don't you make fun of her choice while she's within reach of beating you with her purse?" Holden dared.

"Hell no." Kaige shook his head hard enough to make his dreads swing freely. "I'm not stupid. Amber Brown is a kickass name."

Gavyn hung his head and scratched the back of his head with his free hand, wishing it wasn't so painful to hear it aloud. To remember her smile. To see her resemblance in the tiny human he cradled and wonder if her children would look similarly adorable.

He thanked the universe for introducing him to her. After all, Amber had been the reason he'd finally been able to take sobriety seriously. Losing the best thing he'd ever almost had, well, that was pretty great motivation never to repeat the mistake.

For the first time, he wanted success for himself and believed he had the power to make it happen. A clean life, if a lonely one.

For that, he would always secretly love Amber.

He wasn't sure how long he stood there transfixed by Ambrose. It must have been a while. Eventually the baby fussed a bit and Nola took her to feed. He missed the slight mass in his arms.

When he looked around he spotted the hand-carved wooden rattle set the

Powertools had made for Ambrose. All miniature replicas of the tools her mechanic family used daily. Kaige kept snapping pictures of them with his phone then passing them around for the rest of the Hot Rods to admire. Holden pretended to drill Sabra's nipple with the miniature pneumatic wrench. It was impossible to make the Hot Rods grow up entirely, he thought, as he laughed along with the gang.

Gavyn noticed the daylight fading outside and thought of the things he had yet to do, swinging by the hotel being first on the list, then buying some clothes and essentials to hold him over for a few weeks.

"Hey, Gav?" Sabra called out as he inched toward the door.

"Yeah?"

"Why don't you take this?" Before he could even ask what she meant, she tossed him a steel ring with a single key on it.

"What—?"

"My old place is still under lease. I didn't move any of my furniture either. Haven't had time to sell it with *Hot Rods* and everything else going on. There's no reason you shouldn't crash there." She smiled. "In fact, I'll be insulted if you say no."

"I..." He looked around and found most of the Hot Rods nodding at him. "Okay. Great. This is so awesome. Thank you."

Overwhelmed with their kindness, he didn't know what else to say.

"So you'll swing by the shop tomorrow?" Roman asked him quietly as he was near the door. "Come for dinner. Kaelyn's cooking. It'll be awesome. Then we can talk about your setup after."

"Okay, what time?" Gavyn wondered if he was overstepping. He took a chance anyway. "Ah... Actually, if you want, I don't have anything to do. I'd love to spend my time here on something productive. Maybe there's stuff I could take care of around the garage during the day?"

Quinn—damn, that kid had selective hearing—snuck in another shot, still never looking up from his game. "You can take over my shit. Sweeping sucks. Taking out the trash too. Pumping gas for the hot moms from town who don't want to get messy isn't so bad, though. I'll keep that one—and their tips."

"Better not let Ms. Brown hear you talking like that," Roman reminded his little brother.

"I'll just tell her I heard it from you guys." He grinned and no one had the heart to scold him, since it was definitely true.

He was going to be a heartbreaker someday, Gavyn would bet.

Although he never would have expected it, he couldn't imagine a better outcome from his trip. He'd come to make amends and had ended up with gifts more bountiful than he should receive. Determined, he would earn them.

"So that's okay? I don't mind being on cleanup duty. Anything for you guys, seriously." He cleared his throat. "You don't know how much this means to me."

"In that case…" Kaige raised his brows. "You can be on diaper-changing duty too when we bust out of here tomorrow."

"Nova!" Nola smacked her husband on the shoulder. "You are not foisting your daughter off on company."

"Nope, just her poop." He grinned.

"You better get out of here while you still can." Roman nudged Gavyn. "Otherwise they'll have you cleaning toilets next."

"That might be where I draw the line." He hoped they knew it wasn't true. He'd do whatever he could to pitch in. He owed them that much.

"See you tomorrow, then." Carver waved and the rest of the Hot Rods followed suit.

"Tomorrow," he confirmed.

As he walked out to his motorcycle, he couldn't believe how much more promise the future held than even a couple hours before. He was on the right track and committed to staying there.

With the help of his friends.

CHAPTER TWELVE

"There you are." Amber smiled as she finally caught up with Quinn in the break room of the Hot Rods garage. She'd popped through the side entrance to keep out of the way of the restorations taking place in the main bays and Sabra's filming of the action for their reality TV show. "I've been looking all over for you. I thought you'd be in your room or maybe at the kitchen table like usual."

The teenager shrugged without glancing up from his notes and the open textbook in front of him, which sat beside his laptop. He must be really worried about this test. Buster McHightops was curled up in a doggie bed made out of a tire stuffed with blankets in the corner, fast asleep despite the racket. "Nah. Tom and your mom like to watch *Judge Judy* at four. Figured it would be quieter in here."

The whir of pneumatic tools almost drowned him out.

"What I meant was… There won't be sounds that are tough to concentrate over. The talking on the TV makes it hard for me to read," he covered quickly.

"I'm sure they'd record their shows for after you're done studying," she suggested. Her mother would never make it harder for Quinn to do well in school, not now that he'd only begun to excel.

"It's fine." Quinn shook his head. "Don't want to bug them. This is cool."

"All right." She took a seat next to him and peeked over his shoulder, making a mental note to mention it discreetly to her mom later. "I'm glad you texted me to come over. What are you working on that you thought I could help with?"

He nudged the laptop so that she could see what was on the screen.

"Spreadsheets!" She clapped. "Mmm. My favorite."

Quinn rolled his eyes then said, "You're a total nerd. I knew it."

"Damn straight! Tell me we get to color code stuff too and I'll love you forever." She knocked her shoulder into his as they laughed together. "So what are we organizing here?"

"It's a module on managing finances and budgeting," he explained, then handed her the book with the problems.

"That seems like a super smart skill to teach in high school." She hummed her appreciation.

"Yeah, if I could actually learn it. So far I keep getting errors on my formulas and it's a pain in the ass to line stuff up in these dumb boxes," he grumbled.

"You'll be a pro in time for this test," she promised him.

With her help, they were able to knock out several of the sample sheets in a half hour and she'd even started to teach him some more advanced tricks he could use both for extra credit and in real life. Despite his initial reluctance, he seemed to pick up what she showed him really quickly. Maybe he simply caught on easier from demonstration than reading. She'd have to share that with Tom and her mom for other assignments. Or maybe show Quinn how to check out how-to videos on YouTube if it would suit his learning style better.

While he was typing up a formula, she let her mind wander. That was when she heard voices nearby, growing louder as a couple of guys seemed to be heading this way. She hoped they didn't distract Quinn from his studies.

Roman was talking in his usual soft voice, too low for her to make out his words. A response came from someone whose tone rang deeper.

The sound instantly had her entire body flashing hot then cold.

"Yeah, it's been a shit-ton easier this time around," Gavyn declared, his voice almost regular speaking volume as he neared the break room. "I went to the counselor you recommended at rehab. Plus, any time I have a hint of a craving, I think about how bad I fucked up and I skip wanting to drink and go straight to feeling sick instead."

Amber bolted to her feet, knocking over her chair in the process. There was nowhere to run in the interior space. No windows. No way to escape. She considered ducking beneath the table and hiding. There simply wasn't time.

Gavyn and Roman came through the door in the next instant.

Amber stood rooted to the floor.

He could not have just walked in here! It was not possible that he could be here and no one warned her. They wouldn't do that to her. Unless he'd showed up unannounced?

"Amber!" Gavyn didn't only slam to an immediate stop at seeing her, he also stumbled back a few steps. His face drained of color and the wry smile he'd worn withered into a grimace.

She didn't respond, instead snatching her purse from the table and clutching it to her. If she didn't have to brush by him to leave, she would have darted from the room.

"Shit. I'm sorry. I swear I had no idea you were going to be here. Barracuda promised me you had no plans to visit."

Roman held up his hands. "Don't blame me. She doesn't clear her schedule with Hot Rods. Nola said she wasn't expecting her sister. That's the best I can do."

Gavyn began to retreat from the room. "I didn't mean to bother you."

"Stop!" Quinn stood up as he barked the order, making Buster McHightops pop awake, leap to his feet and growl at nothing in particular. When the dog blinked, stretched then trotted over to Roman and Gavyn with his tail wagging, Quinn continued addressing the guys who'd frozen at his outburst. "*I* asked her to come over. To help me with my homework. I told her you all were busy with a big project."

"You *knew* Gavyn would be here when you texted me?" She whirled toward Quinn, that sneaky little probably-well-meaning runt, and squeaked when she got to Gav's name. It was hard to say. Rusty, since she hadn't uttered it in months.

The kid nodded.

"Shit." Gavyn groaned. "Why would you do that to her?"

Amber's heart slammed inside her chest and her whole body trembled. Seeing him again tore her up. On one hand, he looked so freaking amazing. Cut muscles—visible since he was walking around shirtless—shone with light perspiration exactly like after he'd fucked her senseless. She could guarantee she'd be breaking out her vibrator when she got home. And on the other, every single glance at him tore the scabs off her not-quite-healed heart.

Roman looked at Quinn and frowned. "I know you were trying to do something nice, but this wasn't the right way to go about it."

"He likes her. A lot. I could tell yesterday at the hospital. Couldn't you?" Quinn asked his older brother.

"Yes."

"And *she* misses *him*." Quinn pointed at Amber then back to Gavyn. "She's been sad since the weddings. I hear her crying buckets when she comes to talk to Ms. Brown and I'm in my room. I act like I don't so she doesn't get embarrassed, but—"

"I know." Barracuda thankfully cut him off before he could share any other sensitive information. Still, he didn't try to pretend that

Quinn didn't have the truth of it, and neither did she. Great.

The only way this could get more mortifying was if someone busted her on the number of times she'd gotten herself off to memories of that night—sometimes even coming in her sleep as she dreamed about it— or how often she'd pored over the single email Gavyn had sent her since their disastrous fling had been cut short.

Quinn crossed his arms and stared at the adults like they'd betrayed him. Especially his brother. "You told me that it's okay to fight. But just because you don't like someone's actions doesn't mean you stop loving the person."

"I did say that." Roman nodded.

"So were you lying then or are you lying now?" Quinn's face got red and his hands curled into fists. It wasn't fair to upset him like this when he still worried from time to time about his place in the gang and the stability of the world around him. His abusive past made it hard for him to believe his haven, Hot Rods, could be real and lasting. Easy for him to get confused. Scared. "Gav's not like our mom. He screwed up. Once. He doesn't hate Amber or hurt her all the time or think it's funny—"

Amber had let this go on too long, get too out of hand. It wasn't only her or Gavyn she was impairing now either. "Quinn, please, stop."

She opened her arms and welcomed the teenager into them. He flew against her, wrapping his deceptively strong arms around her in return. A rare thing for him to let anyone touch him or to admit he needed security or reassurance. It only made her feel more like shit.

"I'm sorry, Amber," he muttered against her neck. "I love you like a sister. I want you to be happy."

"I know." She squeezed him tight then held him at arm's length. "And I respect you for doing what you thought was right. I've been silly, letting my hurt feelings stand in the way of making better decisions on how to handle the situation. I'm sorry I set a bad example for you."

"You are?" Gavyn, Roman and Quinn said in unison.

"Yes." She ruffled Quinn's hair. "In the future, how about you come talk to me first and explain how you feel before you do something like this?"

"Okay." Quinn nodded, biting his lip. "So, you're not mad?"

"I'm upset, but I forgive you. And I still love you." She kissed his forehead.

"I'm gonna go..." Gavyn spun around and took one step before she stopped him.

"Don't move," she commanded, and he froze long enough for her to turn back to Quinn. "Now, would it be okay if I talk to him alone for a while since you went to all this trouble?"

"I guess." He smiled somewhat devilishly, packed up his school stuff, then called to his dog. "Come on, Buster. Let's go play fetch."

"Not so fast. I think you and I should have a discussion of our own first." Roman snagged Quinn's collar and steered him toward the door. "You're lucky Amber's so damn nice."

"Uh-oh," Mustang Sally sing-songed as the brothers passed her painting booth. "What'd the kid do now?" When she popped her head out and saw Amber and Gavyn about to faceoff, she gasped. "Holy shit."

"Ugh." Amber groaned. "Close the door, would you?"

Gavyn obliged. "Are you sure you're comfortable being alone with me? Seriously, I'll hit the road. The last thing I wanted was to bother you more. Roman is helping me plan stuff for my bike shop."

"Oh. That's...terrific." She hated the veil of pleasantries between them. Going deeper would hurt. She was scared to dredge up her disappointment and fear. The doubt over what she could have done differently. What might have happened if he'd never wandered from her side that night. "I'm glad to hear you're still doing that."

"Amber." His tone turned pleading, soft and sensual and so damn attractive she hated herself for wanting him even now. "If we're going to do this, can we at least be honest with each other?"

Her head snapped toward him. "I don't think I've ever been anything but with you."

"That's better." He nodded. "It's fine to show me how angry you are. How hurt. I understand. And I'd take it from you if I could."

Amber gave up ground with each baby step he took forward, unsure of her ability to control the fractions of her that wished she could shove him onto the break room table and take things to a place where they fit together so well that none of this pain seemed possible.

Eventually, though, her shoulders bumped into the cinderblock wall. He kept advancing, slow and steady, as if aware of how frightened she was of him and his ability to wound her. When he was a few paces away, he stopped, giving her room to bolt past him if she needed.

She wanted to.

Yet she didn't.

"I'm *so* fucking sorry—" he began.

Amber spoke at the same time, interrupting, figuring she could save them a whole lot of time. "I know. I got your email."

"Oh." He winced. "I sort of hoped I had the wrong address or it went to spam or something, since you never wrote back."

"Nope." She shrugged. "I just...didn't know what to say. Or maybe I wasn't strong enough to type out how I really felt like you did."

"That could either be promising or really horrible." Gavyn's shoulders drew in tight as he tensed, waiting for her to clue him in.

Amber cleared her throat a few times. No sound would come out.

"You're shaking." He put out one hand to cup her upper arm, steadying her and lending her his strength. It was a simple touch. Enough to race through her entire body as if he'd licked her from her head to her curling toes.

When she didn't object, he came even closer, bringing his other hand up to do the same on her other side.

Amber whimpered.

"Are you afraid of me?" he asked, tortured.

"Kind of. Though not how you're imagining." She rested her head on the wall and looked up into his anguished eyes.

"What are you scared of?" he wondered.

"That if I let you walk out of here today..."

"Yeah?" He seemed as horrified by the thought as she was, leaning in to rest his forehead on hers.

"I'm never going to find another man who makes me feel as much as you do." She whimpered, hating the tears bubbling up inside her.

"Amber." He slid his hands behind her, enveloping her in his warm, strong arms. "I've missed you so much. I know I don't deserve another chance with you. But I'm asking for one anyway."

Amber had never wanted to grant someone's wish as much as she did right then. What kind of fool would that make her?

"Tell me you don't sense this connection between us?" He tilted his face down and whispered against her lips, making her melt inside.

Despite every bit of sanity screaming at her to put her hands on his chest and shove—hard, so that she could take a breath not filled with the sandalwood scent of him—she didn't.

Instead, she went onto her toes the barest bit so that their mouths collided.

Neither one of them waited a moment more. They groaned in unison as their lips locked and their tongues began a fierce and desperate dueling match where both of them were, ultimately, winners. Again and again they sipped from each other. For the first time, she had some inkling of what it had to have been like for Gavyn, when he'd stolen that first droplet of champagne on Nola's wedding night.

Because she found herself in the same predicament. Addicted to the rush of passion and pleasure he brought her in the moment, completely discarding the consequences of this indulgence even after he'd proved how devastating they could be.

For that very reason...she should quit him.

"Wait. Gavyn." Amber drew away, hardly able to catch her breath. The lust flooding her system short-circuited every bit of logic she possessed. "This is too much. Too fast. I haven't even really processed the fact that this is really you, here, in Middletown."

"In that case..." He braced his forearms on the wall on either side of her head, as if their kiss has sapped his strength. Willpower, though, he seemed better able to muster because he was calm and collected when he asked, "Will you let me take you out to dinner somewhere fancy so we can talk and get caught up without risking getting *distracted*?"

The way he said it made it clear exactly how they would end up amusing each other if they were left unchaperoned. She didn't doubt it either.

"I'm not sure that's a good idea, Gavyn."

"You just said—"

"I know. But going with impulsive desires didn't work out so well the last time I tried it. Maybe I should be more reasonable now."

He swallowed hard, his eyes closed. "It doesn't have to be a date, Amber. Some time to talk away from everyone else, that's all I'm asking for."

"I shouldn't." She knew better. Right when she thought she would excuse herself from their chat and end this madness, Quinn's accusations came roaring into her mind once more.

Just because you don't like someone's actions doesn't mean you don't still love them.

The image of her mom and Tom followed right after—kept apart by the ghosts in their pasts. Would she regret this moment for the rest of her life if she didn't take the chance to see what might be possible?

It wasn't wise. It wasn't cautious or planned.

She did it anyway.

"Fine. Yes. Let's go. Quick, before I change my mind again." Amber held out her hand and Gavyn clasped it tight.

"Thank you." He gave her a peck on the lips then practically ran for the front of the shop where his bike was waiting, pausing only to snag his polo from the hook he'd hung it on before lending the Hot Rods some elbow grease earlier.

CHAPTER THIRTEEN

Gavyn was grateful that he'd already scoped out restaurants that would, hopefully, impress investors when he got ready to launch Hot Rides. It was easy to mentally select the one that had looked the best and speed off in that direction without having to search online or ask Amber and give her time to back out of their non-date date.

He'd picked up on some of her habits after working alongside her, it seemed.

When she slung her leg over his bike and settled into place against his backside, he knew he was the luckiest bastard in the world. Dressed in slacks, a ruffled maroon blouse and black high heels, she looked entirely too professional to hang around him. The peacock-feather earrings dangling nearly to her collarbones were the sole hint of her adventurous side. They reminded him of the one he'd stolen from her dress to torture her with. Between that and the way she molded to him perfectly, clinging as though they hadn't been split up for months—if they had ever really been together at all—she revved him to the max.

It seemed like only the night before that he'd spent several hours locked inside her.

Or maybe it was her arms, cinched around his waist, that were jogging his memory. Her fingers roamed over his abs and chest for some gratuitous hand holds he didn't mind providing in the least. In fact, he detoured, taking the scenic route to the place he'd selected for his attempt to win her over.

Secluded and romantic, the restaurant used to be a church about a hundred years earlier. It had the original beam ceiling and a wall of stained glass that would be perfectly illuminated this time of day. When Gavyn led Amber inside the foyer, she gasped at the glittering colors cast onto the wide plank flooring.

"I've heard a lot about this place," she said. "I haven't done an event with a budget big enough per head and small enough to fit to consider it a venue contender yet."

"So you've never checked it out in person before?" He asked, pleased to share the experience with her. Their first times together.

She shook her head, making those seductive feathers dance around her shoulders. "I've always wanted to, though. Are you sure you're up for this?"

The nibbles she subjected her lip to nearly drove him mad. Concentrating twice as hard on her question, he thought he knew what she was getting at. "Go ahead. You can say it. Never hold back. You're probably right to worry."

"Okay." She took a deep breath then explained, "They have an extensive wine cellar here. I'd rather go to McDonald's and eat in the PlayPlace ball pit than put you in a dangerous situation. You don't need to impress me to have a chance with me. There are a lot more important things than a fancy meal."

"Like me being able to control my impulses?" It sucked, but he knew she had every reason to be concerned. He hadn't proven to her yet that he was capable of resisting, of overcoming his illness.

These days he had better strategies for coping and he wanted to demonstrate them to her.

She didn't answer. Didn't have to.

Gavyn cupped her face in his hands, glad to see her cheek seemed completely healed. As gently and carefully as he could manage, he delivered an achingly tender kiss to her lush lips, which parted on a soft sigh. Instead of deepening the contact, no matter how badly he wanted to, he released her.

"If I can stop after a single taste of you, then I can handle not drinking here." He took her hand and led her to the inner door, which opened into the main restaurant. "I have a plan. Will you trust me?"

"Ummm…"

It stung that she couldn't yet. That had been asking too much, too soon, he knew. "Fair enough. Maybe tomorrow I'll have earned a little more faith. I'll spend every day doing that until you're comfortable with me again. If you'll let me."

Before she could object, he led her inside.

The moment they walked through the door, Gavyn approached the host. He would have been a hell of a lot more suave about what he was about to do if he didn't *want* Amber to overhear his speech, one he'd prepared, rehearsed and used several times lately to avoid putting himself in a tough situation.

"Good evening. I'm Gavyn. I'll be dining here with my lovely friend Amber tonight. I'm a recovering alcoholic. It would help me out if you could make sure that no wine menus, drink specials, dishes with alcohol or desserts with liquor are offered or served to me, even if I change my mind later."

"Of course, sir. I'll let the staff know about your food allergy." The man smiled broadly and gave him a subtle wink.

"You…" Amber blinked up at Gavyn a few times. "That was…wow."

"I learned from a woman I know that it helps to manage a situation if you're prepared." He smiled at Amber, hoping she wasn't embarrassed he'd revealed his addiction issues to a stranger. It would always be part of him, following them, and maybe that was more than she could handle.

"Thank you for being responsible," she said, beaming up at him. "That's really shrewd of you to head things off."

"I've been paying attention this time around. Actually listening to other people, like Roman, who have made it through the toughest times. Picking up things here and there that I feel like I can use for myself. I go to a local meeting once a week and I'm a member of several online support groups too. I got that tip from one of the other attendees."

"Smart." She squeezed his hand, and he figured she wasn't referring so much to the idea as she was to his involvement in relapse prevention.

At least he hoped that was what she meant.

He paused as they were led through dazzling lights to an intimate table in a glass nook.

"This reminds me of the rainbows at the Hot Rods' weddings." She sighed as she stared at him and the colorful illumination painting his skin. Hers too. It made her even more painfully beautiful than usual.

"I think about that moment a lot, Amber."

"Me too," she agreed with a sad smile. "It helps me sometimes to remember that just when you think things are ruined, they can always turn around."

Afraid to read too much into her statement, he still had to try to show her that he wanted to make things right for her. For *them*, if he could.

"I don't know if you've heard this from your sister, or the Powertools, or Tom and your mom, or whoever. Even if you have, I want you to hear it directly from me too. I haven't touched anything. Alcohol, drugs— nothing...since the night I fucked up." He leaned forward, putting his elbows on the table, screw manners, so that she could see the truth in his eyes. "I never will again. I'm fighting, Amber, every day, and it's becoming easier because I finally get what the stakes are. For the first time since I've admitted I'm sick, there's something I want more than a fix."

He stared at her without daring to say more and scare her off. If she wanted to pretend he was talking about the bike shop, let her. That *was* part of what he meant.

Saved by the waiter, he didn't have to field questions from her about his bold statement. They perused the menu, beverages excluded, and made their selections. When things had quieted down and they were waiting for their meals, Amber cleared her throat.

"If you have something to say, please don't hold back." He hated that he'd stifled some of her newfound recklessness.

"It's just that I've been wondering..." She broke off and stared at the window, which had dulled to a glow as the sun set.

"You can ask me anything," he encouraged.

"Did I do something the night of the wedding to make you unhappy?" she blurted out.

"Amber, no." He nearly knocked the goblet of ice water off the table when he lunged for her hands and wrapped them in his. "You were perfect. *Are* perfect."

"I'm not." She flung the denial at him. "I'm scared. And I'm a shitty friend."

"Hang on. What?" The bombs she was dropping on him had him darting from point to point to avoid impact. There were things being left on the table that he needed to revisit. He compiled a mental list while refusing to interrupt her now that she'd started opening up to him.

"The day we were at the pergola, hanging the curtains..."

"Yeah, I remember it well." A grin crossed his lips despite the tension rolling off Amber.

"Oh jeez. Not that part." She laughed softly and pinched his hand, making him jerk.

He prodded her to continue. "No, seriously, what about it?"

"You told me to let go and promised to catch me if I crashed and burned. I said I'd do the same for you. But when it came down to it, I didn't. I left. I've hated myself every day since then because I didn't fight harder to pick you up, bring you back to a place full of rainbows instead of storms. I'm sorry for that, truly. I was so scared and so hurt. I was weak and I let you down."

A single tear fell down her cheek, breaking his heart all over again.

"If I recall, and I don't really...not totally...I think I didn't give you an option." He winced.

"Sure, you screamed at me. But you were drunk. Or...well, I wish there was a word for how intoxicated you were. *Drunk* doesn't really cover it. I could have ignored you and stuck by you. Ridden in the ambulance with you. Should have. But I was reeling and terrified, which isn't an excuse, really."

"Amber, please. Don't do that to yourself." He lifted her hands to his mouth and kissed her knuckles over and over. "Don't take any of my shit and put it on you."

"All I can do is work on that, like you're doing with your issues." She shook her head. "Because the reality is, I'm still totally freaked out. And confused. I feel like I'm doing the wrong thing if I ignore the progress you've made. At the same time, I have to look out for myself. I don't know how to strike that balance between self-preservation and supporting you."

"Don't worry about it tonight. Enjoy your food and we'll talk and that's all you have to be concerned with, the right now. You know that's another thing they teach us, right? To take things minute by minute."

"I suck at that, remember?" She laughed. "I'll try, though. Seriously, Gavyn, I have to know one thing before I can let it go. Why didn't you fall asleep with me that night? Did you get up to piss or to get rid of the condom and see the champagne Nola had left for me, or was there some other reason you couldn't sleep? Were you already having cravings? Didn't you trust me to help you? Why not wake me up?"

Holy fuck. She'd obviously spent sleepless nights obsessing about something that had been completely out of her control to generate enough options that she could rattle nearly a half-dozen of them off the top of her head. And he was to blame.

In order to salve her conscience, he had to come clean.

"I'm a pussy. I was flipping out."

"Over what?" She tilted her head and squinted at him as if he were joking.

"I wanted more than a fling, but I didn't know how to ask. I thought you would turn me down because...well, I'm a fucking disaster." A shrug and a wry grin fell from him.

"A self fulfilling prophecy." She covered her mouth with one hand, half-laughing yet on the verge of tears. "You know, I fell asleep psyching myself up so that in the morning, I'd admit I hoped we could see each other after the week was out. If I'd only said something right then..."

"It's *not* your fault."

"Everyone keeps saying that to me. That doesn't stop it from feeling like it was sometimes." She sniffled then dabbed her eyes with her napkin.

The food arrived, interrupting them. Rather than ruin their meal with things they couldn't change, they both took a break from the heavy conversation and switched their attention to the decadent indulgences that graced their table in course after course.

Between bites, they talked about easy things like what was going on with the Powertools and Hot Rods. The baby. Quinn, and how he'd be a hell of a man one day. Buster McHightops, Sir Clawdius Fuzzington and their dog-love-cat-hate relationship. Events she had in the works and the new developments on Hot Rides.

He'd forgotten how great it was to share those simple pleasures with her. In no time, they had picked up almost where they'd left off and were proving all over again that they clicked. Big time.

So when they polished off a chocolate raspberry tart for dessert then fell back in their chairs, clasping their full guts, he couldn't help wishing she was on the menu. Making the same mistake as last time wasn't an option. With everything to gain and nothing to lose, he confessed pointblank, "Amber, I still want you. Not only for tonight, but also...for something more."

"Gavyn, I'm sorry. I can't agree to a long-term or committed relationship right now. I still can't believe you're even here. But...I'd be lying if I said I didn't still want you too. You know I do, right?" She put her face in her hand and peeked through her fingers at him as she confessed.

"Yeah, love." He chuckled without malice at her discomfort. "It was pretty obvious when you jammed your tongue down my throat earlier and when your hard nipples were poking holes in my back on the way here."

"Maybe I was cold!" she objected.

"Right. In the middle of summer?" He shook his head. "No. If there's anything I'm sure about, it's that you and I have crazy once-in-a-lifetime chemistry."

"So...what if I don't want to waste that while I'm thinking about the rest?"

If he still had been chewing, he'd have choked and ended their date—because it was *definitely* a date—with Amber giving him the Heimlich maneuver.

"Did you just say you want to sleep with me?" he asked, his pupils dilating as a grin spread across his face, slow and sexy.

"Kind of." She shrugged one slender shoulder. "Fine. Yes. Will you come back to my house tonight, Gavyn?"

"Check, please!"

CHAPTER FOURTEEN

Amber jingled her keys in her palm, noticing how spidery cracks had spread across most of the sidewalk in the past few years as she looked at the house she leased with fresh eyes, wondering what Gavyn would think.

He held the dented screen door as she let them inside then flipped on the overhead light, casting warm, yellowish light on the aged if well-maintained house. Original hardwood stairs stood immediately in front of them with the kitchen off to the right and a tidy living room on the left.

"It's a cute place."

"That's guy code for tiny and so outdated it's practically vintage or retro or something, right?" She laughed, not offended because it was true.

"Hey, anything honestly gained..."

"It's funny, you know. I always dreamed about having a place of my own. Within a few months I went from living with my mom and my sister to Nola moving out and my mom spending most of her time at Tom's." She shrugged with a hint of smile twisting her lips. "It's kind of creepy...and lonely...coming home to a dark, quiet house so often. I'd get a dog, but the landlord refuses to consider it."

Gavyn pulled her into a hug. Resting his chin on the crown of her head, he said, "Well, you're not alone tonight."

"I noticed," she purred as she rubbed herself against him.

"I think that's why I ended up staying at my sister's resort for so long. It felt better being surrounded by people," he admitted.

"You mean you liked checking out all the naked guests, didn't you?" she teased.

"Not *all* of them... The women, sure. I'm not going to lie. The ladies interested in a vacation fling weren't a bad bonus."

"And those who were looking for a wedding fling?" She tried not to be jealous. No such luck.

"Only one of those. She was my favorite." He chuckled even before she poked him in the stomach. Of course, the slab of his abs meant her jab was pretty ineffectual. She'd swear he was even more defined and built than the last time he'd held her this close. Probably true if he used working out as one of his distraction techniques like Roman did.

"So…" Gavyn flipped the lock on the door then faced her. "Your mom isn't coming home tonight, is she?"

"Nope. She packed about a dozen suitcases and hauled her stuff over to Tom's place. Enough to stay for a couple weeks at least so she can be on hand to help Nola with Ambrose. I'm glad I peeked in on them this afternoon before going to find Quinn or I might get my godmother privileges revoked. They turned Mustang Sally's old room into a nursery, though of course the baby is in Kaige and Nola's room for now." She shrugged. "It's a big change…"

"Sometimes those are the best." He stalked closer to her, making her aware of how powerful he truly was despite his tendency to make people feel comfortable around him. That must have been a handy trait in his lawyer days. "Can I be honest, Amber?"

"Of course." She nibbled her lower lip, wondering if he'd changed his mind since he hadn't jumped her yet and his jeans were missing the telltale tent she associated with their fun times.

"I stopped listening when you said your mom wasn't going to bust in on us fucking." He lunged for her, wrapping his hands around her waist and lifting her to him. "The blood started rushing to my cock and now I can't really think about anything except getting inside you again."

Laughing, she looped her arms around his neck and her legs around his waist to help steady herself as he palmed her ass. "I'm a grown woman. I can do as I like without my mom's approval, you know?"

"Yeah, but she's scary as hell and my balls wanted to make sure the coast was clear before they came out to play." He seemed dead serious as he muttered between nuzzles and kisses on her neck. "She and I have an understanding. One I haven't lived up to, remember?"

Then he slowed down, probably thinking too damn much about things other than the steam beginning to rise from where they touched.

Though she wished this was only about sex, she cared. If something was bothering him, she wanted to know. "What's wrong?"

"Sorry." He kissed her light and quick. "I think tomorrow I need to go see her and Tom. To apologize in person. Does she hate me for what I did to you?"

"No." Amber shook her head. "But I'm fairly sure she hates what you did to yourself."

"Are you lying to me, love?"

"No, Gavyn."

"Then what's that look for?"

Maybe it was time to come clean. "My mom and Tom have been encouraging me to respond to your email since about five minutes after it popped into my inbox.

"Now *that* I doubt." He groaned, shaking his head.

"It's true." She leaned in and kissed him sweetly, loving how he turned ferocious, holding her tighter and responding to the demands of his body. "Can we talk about Mom later, Gav?"

"Good idea." He held her still and ground against her core, letting her feel every inch of his steely length, now fully ready to give her another night to remember. "Just one last thing I need to know before I'm all about you."

"Yeah?" She wish he'd hurry.

"What are her favorite flowers?"

"Anything pink." A man who bought her mom flowers? Irresistible.

Amber pushed her fingers into his hair, loving the way the thick strands caressed the sensitive spots between them. She dropped loud, smacking kisses on his chin, cheeks and forehead, hoping he knew how much she appreciated the gesture. Her mom hadn't had a lot of happiness in her life other than her daughters and her recent friendship with

Tom. While that might put some guys off, it seemed to make Gavyn respect her as she deserved.

Smart man.

"Gavyn?"

"Yes, love?" he responded.

"My room is the one at the top of the stairs. There's a full box of condoms in my nightstand."

"I'm on it." He whirled her around and took off, climbing the steep, narrow stairs as easily as if they were a gentle incline and his arms weren't full of willing, squirming woman.

After entering her room, he shut the door and locked it too, pressing her shoulders to the thin faux-wood. "Insurance."

Laughter fell from her in between sighs and soft moans when he used his body to pin her in place and slid his hands beneath her blouse to caress her sides.

"If you were wearing another one of those sexy skirts, I'd have it shoved up and be fucking you against the wall in the next two minutes." He growled against her neck.

"Not without a condom." She shook her head. "Nola already got a lecture for being unsafe, even if it was just once. Despite the fact that I'm starting to understand how she forgot, I don't need to hear that sermon too."

"I'll always protect you," he promised. They both knew he wasn't only talking about contraception. "I haven't given you any reason to believe that, but it's true."

"More fucking, less talking." Amber shook her head to clear out the emotions that were sneaking in past her arousal. That was not what this was supposed to be about.

"Yes, ma'am." He grinned then spun, taking her to the bed before following her down. This time he didn't hesitate to reach behind his back with one hand, grab, then whip his shirt over his head. The plane of his chest attracted her fingers like a magnet. She kneaded the muscles of his pecs and shoulders, her hands tracing the definition between them.

As she followed the indentation down the center of his torso, she caught sight of something on his side. "What's that?"

"Uh..." He didn't look directly at her when he angled toward her so she could see the rainbow that reached from his hip to his ribs. On it, she saw a date. The date of the weddings. And her own initials. "Don't freak out, okay? Please? Pretend like it doesn't mean anything."

For a moment she went cold. Was it right to sleep with Gavyn when she wasn't sure if she wanted something lasting *and* he had feelings for her?

"What if I can't follow through? I don't want to set you back or..."

"Hey, that's for me to worry about." He stroked the hair from her face so he could peer directly into her eyes. "I'm glad to be spending time with you, sharing this with you, even if that's all I get out of it. It's way more than I ever thought I'd have again. Far more than I deserve."

With the tip of one finger, she traced the rainbow. "I can't believe I didn't notice this earlier today."

"I think we were both shocked." He grimaced. "I know for myself, the moment I was in the same room as you again, I couldn't pay attention to anything except trying to make things right. I hope it doesn't bother you that I did it."

Gavyn went quiet, still.

"No, it's...great. I spent a lot of time wondering if maybe that night didn't mean as much to you as it had to me." She hated to admit that.

"You have no idea." He sighed. "That's completely my fault. I won't ever let that happen again. So take a good look then let me get back to stripping you."

Amber leaned forward and kissed the tattoo.

"For the record, the Powertools crew thinks it's hysterical. Neil keeps asking when I'm going to hook up with Roman and the rest of the Hot Rods." He shook his head. "I told them Barracuda's pretty hot and all, but he's nowhere near as smoking as you."

Amber lost it. She grabbed her middle and fell back onto her bed, rolling from side to side as relief, amazement and sheer joy combined to bowl her over. Could this really be happening?

So different from how she'd imagined she'd spend tonight.

So much better.

If that was true, then what was she running from? Why keep pushing him back?

Mind hazed with lust and affection, she couldn't say at that moment. But she was sure she'd come to her senses after a solid orgasm or twenty.

On that note...

Amber's giggles faded when Gavyn kept divesting himself of his clothes, his pants and underwear following his shirt to the floor with a single swipe of his hands. She swallowed hard when his thighs came into view, remembering how he'd thrust into her for hours without ever growing tired. Stamina, he had it.

His high, tight ass and the solid cock he fisted and pumped a few times, slowly, while watching her weren't too bad to look at either.

"Plan on watching me all night, or are you going to join me?" he teased her as he put on a show, licking his palm before stroking himself more vigorously, then cupping his balls and massaging them while he rubbed his other hand over his chest and abs.

"This isn't so bad." Truth was, she couldn't pry her eyes from him long enough to duck out of her clothes. Didn't want to miss an instant of his teasing.

"It isn't for me either." He smiled down at her as if he really meant it, and his stiff cock proved it was no hardship for him to stare at her, even fully clothed. "Except I know how much better the view is about to get."

Pleased, she kicked off her shoes then made quick work of her slacks and underwear. She squirmed on the bed, lifting her ass to rid herself of the unnecessary clothing, leaving herself wearing only a flimsy blouse and a thin lace bra. Somehow, she didn't feel very exposed in front of him.

It might have had something to do with the way he looked at her as if she was a super model instead of an ordinary event planner.

"Get rid of the top."

Amber loved it when he took charge, though she didn't think she'd clue him in to that yet if he hadn't already noticed how wet he made her. With a sweet smile, she did as he instructed, though she inched the fabric slowly up her stomach then her chest before slipping it over her head and tossing it to the floor.

"And the bra."

She reached behind herself and unclasped it without letting it fall away completely, keeping her breasts from his view until he growled ominously. A shimmy helped the fabric glide down her arms and away from her body, leaving her bare for his perusal.

"Fuck." He swiped his hand faster along his cock. "You're more gorgeous than I remembered."

"It was dark that night." She shrugged.

His eyes tracked the rise and fall of her breasts in response.

"I saw you. Clearly. Like I do now." He leaned in and pushed her against the pillows, bearing down along every inch of her.

His fingers snuck between her legs and began to rub her in maddening circles that had her breath coming in broken puffs. He smiled, then kissed her, their mouths matching the repetitive passes of his hand, mimicking the glide and force of his fingers as he prepared her to accept him.

Glad that he didn't plan to make her wait, she flexed her ass, pressing her pussy into his grip more fully.

"Condoms?" he breathed while nudging her belly with the slick head of his cock.

"Top drawer of that nightstand." She pointed, unable to be more coherent.

When he slid open the antique, he hummed. "What do we have here?"

Amber put one hand over her eyes. "I assume you mean my vibrator?"

"This looks a lot fancier than your run-of-the-mill bullet." He plucked her designer rabbit from the drawer. "I think I want to play with it."

"Make sure you grab the lube first. It gets kind of big in the middle. Not sure how your ass is going to take it." She snorted.

"Just for that, I think I'll use this lube after all." He wiggled the bottle at her as he lifted his brows. "On *your* ass, while I use Super-cock to fuck your pussy. That way everyone's happy, right?"

She gasped. "You wouldn't."

"Oh, Amber." He laughed. "Fuck yeah I would. Will. You'll like it. I promise."

When she didn't respond right away, he brought his new finds with him and crept closer.

"Does that turn you on?" Gavyn monitored her every reaction for the answer.

"I guess..." What the hell? Why not be honest? Not like it was a secret. "I've kind of wondered, you know, since Nola started hooking up with more than one guy at a time. Seems like it could be kind of hot if you were into that sort of thing."

"You're not, right?" He seemed genuinely concerned. "I don't know if I could share you, Amber. I'd be more likely to chop a guy's hands off if he tried to touch you. Hell, if he so much as *looked* at you naked. I'm kind of possessive about the things I love."

Whoa.

That was not the same as *I love you*, she promised herself. He didn't just drop the L bomb like that. She loved mango gummy bears. That didn't mean she was *in* love with them.

Still, he didn't try to correct the possible misconception. He simply stared into her eyes and waited for her to respond.

"Good, because I don't think that's my thing either. But...like you said...with you playing all the parts..."

"We'll get around to that." He smiled as he kissed her deep and slow. "First I want to feel your tight pussy hugging my cock again."

"In favor." She nodded, reaching for him when he didn't move fast enough to suit her.

Gavyn smirked as he opened the condom and rolled it on, much more slowly than necessary.

"Is that payback for my striptease?" she wondered.

"Only the beginning of it, yes." He grabbed her legs beneath her knees then yanked, sending her sprawling on her back, completely open to him and eager to welcome him into her body once more.

The wash of his might and authority over her was more arousing than the sight of him ready and willing to fuck her senseless. That was saying something.

Gavyn fit himself to her and remained kneeling so they both had a clear view of themselves fusing once again. Or would, if he'd ever finish the job and impale her.

"Tell me again how you want things between us to move in slow motion?" he goaded.

"Not *this*." She reached for his flanks to yank him to her.

In a flash, he snagged her wrists in his hands and forced them to the pillow on either side of her head, sinking lower in the process so that they were totally aligned.

Amber swallowed hard and closed her eyes, feeling the weight of responsibility float away from her. She willingly surrendered to him and the decadence he was about to treat her to.

"That's right, love." He nuzzled her ear, whispering praise as he rewarded her with an inch of his cock, then another and another. "Take me. All of me."

So she did.

Her legs spread wider, allowing him to fit into the V of her thighs, penetrating her deeper with every movement. Before she could quite relax enough to stretch comfortably around him, he'd filled her to capacity and then a bit more.

"You're so fucking tight, Amber," he groaned before retreating a fraction of an inch then reintroducing himself to her over and over until the strokes became liquid and graceful. Each one caused his body to tap her clit, making her groan.

Already, she began to rise toward climax. She could tell it would be the desperate kind that would leave her needier after a quick, hard release. Somehow, so could he.

"Go ahead, come on my cock," Gavyn dared her. "Let's get the first one out of the way so that you can really enjoy it when I take you higher."

As if she had a choice when he combined dirty talk with the sinful arc of his hips, fucking her exactly as her body demanded. She clawed his back, afraid and relieved simultaneously when the typhoon of emotions and desire he inspired hit her all over again, like it had three months ago.

Even better now, really, because she had thought she'd never experience this crazy lust again in her life. Especially not with the man smiling into her eyes, bringing her down from the pinnacle of rapture while still promising her more.

"Have you ever taken it in the ass, Amber?" he growled against her ear.

"No," she admitted.

"Played with yourself there?"

"Nope."

He groaned. "I'll go slow. Swear you'll let me know if I'm hurting you."

When she looked into his light brown eyes and nodded the barest bit, he stole one more kiss then withdrew, making her groan at the emptiness he left behind.

"I'll fix it in a minute, love." He placed a kiss on her clit then nudged her hip. "Roll over. Get on your knees for me again. Do you have any idea how fucking hot you were like that?"

She answered with a moan.

"It'll go easier if I'm seated inside you first, before we get fancy." He surprised her by nipping the fleshy part of her ass on the left then spanking the right side.

Neither of them said out loud what she was thinking—how easy it was to trust him here, like this, in bed. If only she could say the same when it came to something more than sexual gymnastics.

Gavyn opened the lube and slick sounds followed. She was startled when it was something warm instead of cool that pressed against her back passage. Was he licking her?

God, he was.

She gasped and tried to hold still. It was impossible to maintain her position with the riot of awareness he instigated in her never-before-stimulated nerve endings.

The deep, knowing chuckle he gave against her skin didn't help at all. "I told you it would be good.

His smart mouth was followed by his finger, now slicked in gel that had come up to temperature against his skin. While he continued to kiss, lick and nip her lower back and the swells of her ass, he bored inside her with the thickest damn fingers a man had ever possessed. Or at least that was what it felt like.

A grunt escaped her as he caused burning that began to deaden the pleasure he'd granted her first.

"Relax, love."

"Easy for you to say." Amber gritted her teeth.

"It is, because it will make this more enjoyable for you, and that's what I will always want." He hypnotized her with his steady, low murmuring and the constant pressure of his massaging finger.

Eventually, she felt him making progress and stopped holding her breath.

Her muscles relented somewhat, allowing him to tunnel farther inside. When she thought she'd felt as many new and wondrous things as possible for one evening, he flipped to his back, with his head between her legs, his finger still partly embedded in her, and began to lave her clit.

Amber shuddered, allowing him to have his way with her. Soon she forgot about the slight pain and relished the brilliant pleasure he gave her instead. That was when she realized he had fit his entire finger in her then added a second, which worked her open while his tongue continued to distract her.

He paused long enough to praise her and add, "Your pussy is tight, but this... Damn, Amber, you're going to kill me. So hot."

He punctuated every phrase with a twist of his fingers, spreading them apart then bringing them back together, and when he resumed twirling her clit with the tip of his tongue, she couldn't resist falling into another climax.

By the time she'd finished shuddering, he had mounted her, his cock now aimed at her ass rather than her pussy. Eager to give him some echo of the bliss he'd imparted, she rocked back.

Instead of taking him inside her, she got the flat of his palm on her butt, hard enough to really sting. "That's not how this is going to work. I'll give it to you as I see you can take it. Not faster. I won't hurt you again, Amber."

She decided it was probably wise not to mention her glowing ass cheek unless she wanted the other to match, which didn't sound entirely unpleasant as the heat coursed through her veins, enhancing the lingering delight effervescing through her system.

True to his word, Gavyn concentrated on molding himself to her, merging them in the most painless way possible. This time she felt none of the discomfort and only pure, unadulterated lust.

Fully seated, he leaned forward, hugging her to his chest and raking his teeth down her neck. "You're everything I could want. You fit me like you were made for me."

Amber whimpered, because although she didn't care to admit it out loud, she felt the same about him. "Fuck me, Gavyn. Please."

"Such pretty begging, but no, not yet." He nibbled on her earlobe when she made a sound of protest. "We're not finished. I'm not going to last long in this sexy ass and I want to see your toy in action too."

She'd already forgotten about the vibrator. Who needed it when she had a living, breathing sex god filling her?

Gavyn rotated until he reclined against the headboard and held her on his lap. Probably for the hell of it, or possibly because he couldn't resist a sample of what was to come, he lifted her then let her sink onto his shaft a half dozen times before trapping her to his body again.

"Oh God." Her head fell onto his shoulder, rocking to the side when his mouth searched for hers until they could exchange swipes of their tongues and lips while her ass clenched around his pulsing cock.

With her eyes closed, she didn't see it coming.

Gavyn had reached between them. He inserted the toy into her channel, making both of them groan as it nudged his cock through the thin barrier of tissue separating them.

"Holy shit!" she yelled at the fullness of it.

"Too much?" he asked quietly, one hand plumping her breast while the other tapped the end of the toy, hammering it against her lightly.

"Not enough." It would never be enough if it felt this good.

He laughed softly.

When he pressed the top button, turning on the vibrator portion of the rabbit, he jerked and cursed in her ear. "That might be too fucking good."

"Yes, it might. For me too. Don't feel like you have to hold out this time, Gavyn." She had loved it so much when he'd surrendered and come with her. Almost more than the absurd pleasure he'd gifted her with. Solo orgasms were nothing compared to release accompanied by him.

"What's this other button do?" he wondered a moment before he pressed it.

Neither one of them could stay still then. Amber rolled her hips, driving both the toy and Gavyn deeper, as far as they could get.

"It moves? The whole shaft is rotating. I'm pretty sure my dick would break if I tried that." In awe, he told her what she could damn well feel herself. No other time that she'd used the toy had it ever made her feel like this—full to bursting with its surging shaft accompanied by the pressure of Gavyn's cock spreading her ass, massaging her deep from within.

The portion of the vibrator, the actual floppy bunny ears, that remained outside her body provided external stimulation to her clit, buzzing in precisely the right place.

"Gavyn!" she screamed.

"Fucking, fucking—" he said then began to move within her tight clutch. "Jesus. I'm fucking—"

Amber braced herself with her hands on the pillows on either side of his torso, holding herself up as well as she could to give him room to maneuver.

While he pressed into her ass, grinding up into her, he reached around and fondled her chest, pinching one of her nipples. Every pleasure point in her body was stimulated by his presence in, on and around her.

She tipped her face to the side so he could kiss her. Endlessly, or at least it seemed they stayed that way for a long time, doing as much as they could to hang on to the rapture that pushed them toward the edge of orgasm like a massive tidal wave.

"I can feel you tightening," he groaned into her parted mouth as her ability to respond degraded and all she could do was hang on for the ride. "You're going to make me come so hard, I'm going to fill this fucking condom."

"Gavyn!" she shrieked.

"Fuck. Yes." He grunted then, the edges of his control fraying as they rocked together then apart while the vibrator danced inside her, thrilling them both.

The closer she came to exploding, the more stretched she felt. The intense pleasure made it almost too hard to unravel.

"Oh no." Gavyn bit her lip, sucking it in his mouth before ordering. "You will not bail now. You're coming with me. I'm not going to be the only one fucking losing his mind tonight."

That much she could give him. He would have no doubt of their ultimate compatibility in bed or how much he satisfied her.

His escalating thrusts in her ass meant he pounded into the vibrator, making it tap against her clit in some kind of lusty Morse code that translated to something like COME COME COME.

So she did.

Amber arched, relying on Gavyn to catch her when her body flew into auto-response and quit obeying her brain. She let sensation flood each cell of her body and her mind whited-out on ecstasy. Somewhere far away, she heard him groaning and cursing, bellowing her name as he pumped into her in time to the spasms of his corresponding orgasm.

The release was complete and even more potent than the ones they'd shared before.

Amber checked out for a while. She floated on the endorphins that cycled through her organs, riding the wave of euphoria he had generated for them. When she came to, Gavyn was holding her tight. He seemed as wrung out as she was, but he kept talking, low and soft as if he realized she needed time to regain her composure.

"I was a completely idiot, love," he muttered. "This time I plan to stay where I belong, wrapped around you...all night long."

Goose bumps broke out along Amber's arms, rousing her from her delighted trance. Where she'd been warm a moment ago, now she shivered.

Because if he stayed the night, holding her as she slept and waking her with gentle, morning lovemaking, she would never have the strength to keep things casual between them.

"Gavyn." She winced.

"Yeah, love?" The way he reverently trailed his fingertips across her bare skin didn't make it any easier for her to continue.

"I'm not ready for that." He froze when she sat up, drawing the sheets around her.

"What?"

"This was supposed to be physical fun only, remember?"

The pinch of his lips and the crinkle around his eyes that he quickly masked didn't make her job any easier. She had to have time and space to think. "You're kicking me out?"

"I need you to go." She nodded, her eyes filling with tears.

Gavyn's expression went flat. Still, he didn't fight. "Okay, love. Please don't cry. Please. I don't like it. But I'll do it. Whatever it takes to give you only pleasure. Only joy."

He leaned in and kissed her one last time, with so much tenderness and reverence that she nearly caved and begged him to ignore her request.

Before she could, he broke away, disposed of the condom then drew on his clothes. When he was fully dressed, if adorably mussed, he leaned in and murmured, "Let me tuck you in at least."

She nodded.

"There's a spare key in the bowl on the entryway table," Amber told him. "Will you lock the deadbolt on your way out?"

"If I get to keep the key to your house." A ghost of his smile returned.

"For now." Turning onto her side, she snuggled into her pillow, her heart heavy and her body still humming with relief despite the anxiety infringing on it.

"Good enough." He bent down and pressed his lips to her forehead, made his way to the door, turned off the light and whispered. "Thank you for giving me another chance, Amber. Sleep well. Dream dirty things about me."

"Good night, Gavyn." Amber waited until she heard the purr of his chopper cruising down her street at a surprisingly reasonable speed before she closed her eyes.

If a few tears leaked out to dot her pillowcase, she ignored them, telling herself she'd done the right thing. Taken things slow. Kept herself from getting hurt again.

But if that was true, then why was she crying?

CHAPTER FIFTEEN

The next afternoon, Gavyn sat in the garden behind Tom London's house, nursing his third glass of iced tea, which was no longer much more than mostly melted ice cubes. Eli's dad was kicked back in a hammock that stretched between two trees, overlooking a water feature. Natural hardscaping made it seem as if a waterfall originated at a rough-hewn rock wall then spilled along the meandering garden stream into a pond filled with koi.

It reminded Gavyn of his used-to-be-favorite place at Bare Natural.

He hadn't been able to bring himself to revisit the spot since that fateful morning he'd been found there, but he appreciated the Hot Rods' version of the relaxing environment and was glad to have something similar he could still enjoy without revisiting the exact site of his worst failure.

He'd spent the past hour telling Tom about the industrial real estate he'd toured that morning, including the property he already had his heart set on. It was only a half-mile down the road and had everything he needed to transform it into Hot Rides.

"So you put a bid in on the old Hendry place?" Tom steepled his fingers over his abs.

"Yeah." Gavyn nodded. "They said I should hear something pretty quick. I guess it's been on the market a while."

Could it happen that fast? That perfectly?

"I think it's been about four years since they retired and moved to Holiday, Florida. Haven't heard a single word from them since. Must be nice down there," Tom supposed.

Afraid to get his hopes up, Gavyn rattled the ice in his glass then tried to tease a few more drops from the depths. As if she could sense his nervousness about the deal falling through, Ms. Brown changed the subject.

"Well, are you two ever going to get to the good stuff?" she asked Gavyn from where she sat on a blanket, her back resting against one of Tom's hammock trees as she gave him a gentle push, setting him swinging every now and again.

The cheery flowers Gavyn had brought her were tucked against a rock nearby, their stems drinking from the pond temporarily. None of them had been ready to leave the beautiful afternoon sun for the confines of the house.

"Hmm?" He pretended not to understand, since he wasn't sure if he was ready to take this conversation where he knew it was about to go. *Had* to go.

"Don't play dumb, son." Tom shook his head. "Best to get it over with and tell Mama Bear what she needs to hear before she forgets her Southern manners and tears you limb from limb."

"Oh, um." He scratched the back of his head, unsure of where to begin.

"Our landlord called this morning about a guest with a loud motorcycle who left awfully late last night, making crabby Mrs. Darlington bitch up a storm at him this morning. So I guess all I really need to know is if you plan to treat my daughter with the respect she deserves." Ms. Brown didn't flinch as she stared at him, monitoring his reaction. "That means taking care of yourself too if you're supposed to be the person who has her back."

"I—well, yes, ma'am." Gavyn wasn't sure how exactly to answer her since he was still trying to pretend like he hadn't just gotten remotely busted with his pants down. Sort of.

"Mom!" Amber scolded from where she appeared around the corner of the house, as if she had just come in from the parking lot out front, or maybe from visiting her sister and Ambrose. With one hand on her hip and indignation flaring in her eyes, she looked like a warrior princess, which he loved. "I can manage my own relationships."

"Uh oh." Tom attempted to rock out of his hammock, probably to hustle into the house. Ms. Brown put her foot up and kicked the edge of his swing. The jolt set it in motion and tumbled the garage owner into the netting, where he rode out the wave. It was that or bust his ass.

Or have it busted for him if he tried to evade the mother-daughter fracas about to unfold.

So Gavyn didn't bother trying to make a hasty exit of his own.

Instead, he risked being maimed and held out his hand to Amber as she neared. "There's no reason to hide how I feel. It's fine if she wants to make sure my head isn't up my ass anymore. I told you, Amber, and I'll tell your mom or anyone else who wants to know that I'm determined to show you I can be a better man. For you."

"I think it might be more effective if you were as interested in self-preservation," she said as she joined him on the bench.

"I am. Inviting you to share my life is the best thing I could do for myself." Unconcerned with their audience, he reached over and lifted her up, scooping her into his lap.

She didn't fight, so he took that as a good sign.

It seemed they were destined to air their business. He didn't mind if it meant she could talk through how she felt with him and two of the people who were most important in her life. He didn't blame her for being confused after the way things had gone. If this is what it took to help her over it, he would.

"I spent a lot of time last night thinking," she admitted. "I almost called you about a thousand times. Either just to talk, or to ask you to come back. That's why I kept stopping myself. Because I don't know if I can resist falling into something with you when I'm not sure that's wise."

"It's okay. I understand." Gavyn would give her as much time as she needed to see he was serious about her and the path he could see for them.

"Usually I know what to do. I can weigh the pros and cons and pick an option. When it comes to you, I can't sort it out. I've tried. I've spent so much time thinking about it and I can't make up my mind about what's best." Her voice wavered.

"You know, honey, I think it might be you who needs an intervention these days." Ms.

Brown aimed her well-meaning ire at her daughter. "You know damn well what you've decided in your heart. We've talked about this enough times that I've read it in your eyes. Gavyn screwed up. Big time. We all know that, no one more than him. You're not unsure, you're scared. I get that, Amber. You know I do, and I worry for you too. But I think it might be time to stop adding up the facts and take a chance. You have to have *faith* in people you love sometimes. You don't care for someone because you can see the future and know that they've proven they're going to stick by your side. You do it because you *believe* they're deserving when you hand over your heart. It might not last. You might get hurt again. There are no guarantees in life, Amber. It's scary and risky, but...I truly believe you'll be better off—have *lived* more—for having taken the chance. Go ahead, baby, knowing I'll always be here to do what I can if life disappoints you."

Tom was looking at Ms. Brown like she'd grown three heads. Gavyn wondered why, but he wasn't about to derail the woman by asking since she was arguing in his favor.

Before Amber could refute her mother's opinion, he kissed her softly and hoped to sway her toward seeing things their way. "Please, love, give me a legitimate second chance. I can't promise I'll never let you down, though I swear I'll do my best to deserve you every day. Not only in bed, but in your life and your heart."

"La la la!" Ms. Brown jammed her fingers in her ears and pretended to drown out his talk of their prior arrangement.

Tom, however, grinned. He tossed them a mocked salute. "Good job, kid."

"Well, how can I argue with all that?" Amber offered him a watery smile. She took a deep breath, nodded, then said, "I'd actually already come to that conclusion myself around the time my alarm went off this morning. I'm not entirely sure I'm doing the right thing... If you can be patient when I get scared, I want to try."

"That's all I can ask." He hugged her tight.

"Okay, Gav. Let's test this thing out and see where it takes us."

"Really?" He grinned so huge he was afraid his mouth would split open.

"Yeah." Amber wrapped her arms around his shoulders and hugged him tight. "I'm so glad you came here. Everything will work out. I really am starting to believe that."

As if fate had a funny way of knowing precisely when to intervene in Gavyn's life, his phone buzzed in his pocket. He wedged his hand between him and Amber to retrieve it.

"Oh, I thought you were happy with my decision." She pouted.

They all laughed, even her mom, when he turned red then peeked at the screen.

"It's the realtor." He did a fist pump.

"Go ahead, answer it," Tom urged him, as if he was going to let the call go to voicemail.

Brimming with optimism, he put it on speaker before he picked up. "Hello?"

"Gavyn." The realtor had sounded a lot perkier this morning. Maybe she wasn't an afternoon person.

"Hey. Did you hear back already?" He smiled over at Ms. Brown.

"Yes. The Hendrys agreed to the price in your offer."

"That's fantastic!" He squeezed Amber with his free arm, thrilled when she squealed and smooshed him back just as easily.

"Unfortunately—"

Something heavy and hard dropped into his gut like a dead engine. He didn't bother to say anything, waiting for the bad news.

"I tried every single mortgage broker I know. No one was willing to back the loan. For a self-employed person, they require two years of steady work history and a stable personal profile."

"Wait." He knew what she was saying in professional code. "You mean they won't sign the title over to an addict."

"I'm sorry, Gavyn." She seemed embarrassed, probably irritated to be put in the middle and have done all that work for exactly zero commission. "If you have a partner, someone—"

"I don't." He tried not to snap at the messenger. It was tough. "I won't make anyone else responsible for my statistically likely fuck-ups."

"Give me a call back if something changes," she said.

"It won't. Thank you, and sorry for wasting your time."

He clicked the end button before he could humiliate himself more in front of his new girlfriend—if she still wanted him after that—and her parents.

For a moment, no one spoke.

Then Tom tried to bridge the gap. "It's only a hurdle, son. Why don't you talk to Eli and the rest of the guys at the shop? I bet they'd be more than willing..."

"They've been kind enough already." He shifted Amber onto the seat beside him, then stood.

"Gavyn, wait," she called to him as he headed for his bike and the open road. He should have known better than to let himself hope. "Please."

"I need some time to clear my head. Figure out something else." He was afraid there weren't any other options. After all, wasn't he on Plan Q at least by now?

The reminder that he wasn't, and never would be, good enough for her—that his past would always define him—was another burr agitating him.

"I'll go with you. I can help," she offered. "I have a bunch of contacts around the city through my business. Let me talk to some people. Aren't we in this together? Don't shut me out."

"I can do it on my own. I'm not going to put your reputation on the chopping block for my own gain. Thanks, Amber, but... I gotta go." Couldn't she see that if he stayed he'd lose his calm and the last shreds of his dignity along with it?

"Okay." She bit her lip as she dropped her outstretched hand. "Will I see you tonight?"

"I'm not sure." He didn't know what else to say. Promises were beyond him at the moment.

"Don't prove them right, Gavyn," Ms. Brown said softly, barely loud enough for him to hear as he left the garden. He lifted his hand in a goodbye without turning around.

CHAPTER SIXTEEN

Amber watched Gavyn go with a sickness in her gut that was a paler version of the loss she'd experienced when she'd seen EMTs load him into an ambulance while she stayed behind. He was hurt, maybe more so right then than he had been months ago, and she was doing nothing to assuage his pain.

Worse, his rejection of her help had her waffling. Had she made the right decision?

"Take a deep breath, Amber," her mom advised.

So she did. Several times in a row.

When she could think above the panic attempting to choke her, she realized what she had to do. If she was committed to this route, there was only one solution for them both. It wasn't fair to proclaim to be his life partner with only a half-assed belief in him. No one could succeed under those circumstances.

Amber refused to hinder Gavyn. She wanted to help, to do everything in her power to make his efforts—both business and personal—a success. Only then could they both thrive. He would do the same for her, she was sure of it.

"Well..." Her mom looked at her with her eyes bugged out. "What are you waiting for?"

"What do you mean?" Amber rubbed her temples, unsure if she had the strength to endure another scolding right then.

"I know my daughters. You've got that look in your eye. Like you have a plan."

"I might." She grinned, though it faded when she thought of how vehemently Gavyn had objected when Tom suggested he ask the Hot Rods for assistance. Or when she'd offered to call around for him.

"Spit it out!" Her mom waved her hands, exasperated.

"*I* want to do it. I'm going to co-sign the mortgage."

"I knew I raised you right." Her mother smiled softly.

"Mom, he didn't want someone else to sign. Maybe he doesn't like the idea of having a partner..."

"No." Willie shook her head violently. "You've got it right. Don't doubt yourself so much just because the last time you gambled, you lost. Tom suggested that the Hot Rods would put themselves on the line. You recommended a stranger do it. That's totally different than if you were to step up. Not as the head of Brown & DuChamp, but as Gavyn's lover. I can't say I'm not worried—I'm your mom, after all. But if this is what you think is right, then you should trust your instincts, baby. You've got good ones. Believe in yourself enough to do what you know you should. And if it doesn't work out, we'll be here for you."

"I want to do it. You know I've been looking for investments outside the company for diversification. We've got spare cash and, frankly, I do believe he's going to make a killing. Having ridden on one of his bikes, I can say on his own it was likely. With the Hot Rods affiliation, it's a no-brainer. Besides, this kind of property holds its value. Co-signing isn't a risk to Brown & DuChamp, only to my ego." And her heart, though she didn't say that aloud. Amber truly feared a misstep and what that could do to her fragile, budding relationship with Gavyn. "Unfortunately, I still don't think he'll accept my help."

"Men can be pretty dense sometimes." Tom shrugged one shoulder. "Gavyn's no exception. He thinks he's keeping you out of his mess if he doesn't bring you into things.

What he hasn't realized yet is that if you're a pair, you share the same problems. It's okay to be afraid, Amber. Things are new, happening fast, and you got off to a terrible start. I admire how brave you are to put yourself out there again on a personal level. Your mom and I both understand how nearly impossible that is. I'd guess that the connection between you and Gavyn has to be the strongest of any of the kids to fall in love around here lately for you to even consider going out on a limb like this. I also believe you're reading the situation exactly right. Gavyn's trying his hardest, knocking down every obstacle in his way, and he deserves a break. You can be his solution."

"So you don't think it's dumb—"

Her mom cut her off. "Nope. You've always been smart. And one aspect of intelligence is learning from your mistakes. How many times have you told me that if you could rewind your life, you'd stick by him the morning after the weddings?"

"Once or twice." She grimaced, knowing it was easily a hundred.

"So this time, don't take no for an answer. He's hurt and turning inside himself. It's not productive and it's not healthy. Don't let him get away with bull like that. I'd kick his ass if he left you to stew when you were down. Get on the phone and tell that woman what you want. Co-sign for Gavyn's mortgage, but make it a fair deal. He's not a charity case." Her mom gestured wildly as if she was dense. "Treat him like a responsible man, and he'll act like one. If he doesn't...well...I'm sure you'll think of something."

Had her mom implied that she use sex to her advantage?

Amber looked at Tom to get his take. He was grinning. "I love hanging around this place. It's never dull with you kids. Your mom's right. If you can fix this for both of you, maybe you'll start to believe that the two of you can be strong enough to overcome the shit life tosses at you if you're willing to stick together. I can't imagine a better cure for your fear, honey."

She swallowed hard, looking between two of the people she trusted most in the world. If they thought it was a good idea, and her heart thought it was a good idea...

Amber closed her eyes, drew a deep breath and jumped.

So much for careful, or rational, or planned.

"I'm going downtown to talk to her in person. It's Christine from Huntington Real Estate, right?" She recalled something Roman had mentioned earlier, when she'd stopped by the shop on her way over here.

"Yup," Tom confirmed.

"Call us if you need anything." Her mom blew her kisses.

Amber didn't stop there. She jogged over, clutching her mom to her for a second, then did the same to Tom before she trotted out to her car.

"Good luck!" he yelled right before she was out of hearing range.

***

Amber's hands were shaking when she lifted her fist to rap on the door to Sabra's old apartment. Gavyn's motorcycle was parked in the lot below, so she figured he was simply ignoring her when he didn't answer right away. At least it was better to concentrate on that than the nightmare scenarios she could cook up. She gave a second knock, louder this time, and was relieved when his footsteps neared.

"Amber?" His voice rose in pitch and his body went tense as his eyes widened.

Was it because he was doing something—drinking, drugs, *something*—that he didn't want her to see? Or because no one had ever bothered to ignore him when he got all blustery and solitary?

She didn't smell alcohol on his breath.

Prepared for the worst, but hoping for the best, she asked, "Can I come in?"

"I'm not in a very good mood." He cracked the door wider. Still, he didn't move out of the way far enough for her to enter. For the span of a few heartbeats, she was completely distracted by his lack of a shirt.

His ripped chest and abs always made her hands greedy to touch something so fine.

She gave her head a shake then peeked around behind him.

"What're you looking for? A pile of empty bottles? Lines of coke on the coffee table?" He groaned then flung the door wide. The only indulgence she spotted was an open pizza box and a can of soda. "I'm not using, Amber. I'm just fucking disappointed. Humiliated. I got my balls handed to me today in front of my girl and her mother. Hell...parents, counting Tom. No biggie."

Clearly it was to him. So would he freak when he realized what she'd done?

Maybe it hadn't been such a good idea after all.

"I'm sorry." She was. She hated that she doubted his ability to stay clean, even for a moment. Her sense of self-preservation was going to take a while longer to get up to speed with her heart. "I'm not going to lie—I'm worried about you. Not in a critical way, though. It's more like I want to offer my support through what I know will be a difficult time. That's what your groups would tell you, right? To find someone to lean on? To accept freely offered help when you need it? If we're going to have a relationship, I expect you to do the same for me when I'm down. And I don't have a single doubt that you will. Ultimately, that's what made me change my mind about giving us a chance. We're stronger together, Gavyn."

"Shit, you're right." He hunched his shoulders, refusing to fall into old traps for long. "I know it's going to take time for you to see that I'm serious about sobriety. I'm fine with you checking in with me on how I'm handling things. More than that, I appreciate your support. It's just hard sometimes to accept..."

He reached for her then, and she flew into his arms, holding him tight.

"It felt like such a slap in the face when I heard the realtor say not one person believed in me enough to take a chance." He groaned into her hair. "I know no one can see the changes in me, but they're real. I'll keep proving it day after day until the reservations are gone. Forever if I have to. Sometimes it saps all the energy I have, though."

"On those days, I hope you'll lean on me," she whispered in his ear. "Like you are now. I'm here for you. I'll do my best to pick you up and make you feel like the amazing man you are."

"Does that mean you'll give me a BJ?" He winked down at her. "That always makes me feel like a stud."

"Maybe." She rolled her eyes at him. "But I thought you might like something else first."

Amber tugged her messenger bag around to her front then flipped open the pouch. From a neat folder inside, she withdrew a fat manila envelope and handed it to him.

"What's this?" He looked at her rather than opening it.

"The paperwork you need to sign to complete the purchase of the Hot Rides garage."

"Are you joking?" His hand flew to his forehead, rubbing the wrinkles that appeared there when his brows drew together. "I—"

Gavyn shook his head. It was weird to see such an eloquent guy speechless. She prayed it was because he was thrilled and not because he was pissed.

Amber gambled and stepped closer, going onto her tiptoes to kiss his cheek. "All you have to say is, 'thank you', and then sign on the million dotted lines I marked with those *sign here* sticky notes."

"I can't accept—"

"You can, actually." She put her finger on the tip of his nose and smirked. "Just so you know, that would make us partners. I would get a twenty-percent share in Hot Rides."

"So it's not a handout?" Eyes gleaming, he began to smile and reached for her.

"Maybe a hand up, but mostly it's simply good business." Amber shrugged. "What can I say? I believe in you. In your ideas and your capabilities. I want in on the action."

"Love, I'll give you all the action you require." He grinned. "Is that part of the agreement too?"

"Nah. Let's call it my signing bonus."

"I thought you didn't believe in mixing business and pleasure?"

"That was before I met you. You've changed a lot of things about me." That was more true than he probably realized. "For the better."

Amber shrieked then cracked up when he swept her into his arms and spun her around until they were both dizzy. He collapsed into a slouch on the couch and she ended up straddling him, peering up into his handsome face.

"I can't believe you would do that for me." His fingers were gentle as they combed her hair into place. "This will bind us together, you know?"

"I'm hoping." She tossed her hair back with a shake of her head.

"Hmm, now that you mention it, I *did* notice how much you liked it when I used my tie on you at the cabin..." His eyes narrowed as he studied her closer. "But seriously, this is the nicest thing anyone's ever done for me. I will never be able to repay you."

"You already are and you will continue to every day that you're happy—a fulfilling part of my life."

"Does that mean you still want to go out with me?" he asked.

"Were you thinking you were going to be able to take back what you said earlier?" One brow raised as she dared him to change his mind.

"Hell no. In fact... Ms. Amber Brown," he murmured between sweet kisses as his hands roamed over her back and ass. "I think you should know that I love you. I'm pretty sure I have since the moment you kneed me in the nuts three months ago, but I was being cautious, since I know you like that approach so much."

She laughed down at him, drawing him in for another sweep of their mouths against each other before she responded. "Well, Gavyn. I think *you* should know that I've decided to be reckless and wild. At least with you. Because if you can't take some calculated risks with the person you love, then who else can you do it with?"

"The only person you'll be doing *it* with from now on is me." He growled then bit her neck, hopefully leaving a mark in the process.

"I think I can agree to those terms." With her face upturned, she beamed at him.

Gavyn stood, picking her up as he did. He turned and headed for the bedroom at the back of the apartment. "In that case, I believe a celebration is in order."

She whooped as he strode along the hallway, eating up the distance with his long gait. When they reached the bedroom, he let her thighs slip out of his grasp, allowing her to slide down his hard body. Within moments, he'd snatched the hem of her lilac sundress then whisked it over her head. The fashion scarf around her neck fluttered to the floor, leaving her standing before him in a delicate floral bra and panty set.

"They say the only time a woman wears matching underwear is when she plans on getting laid." He smirked. "Had high hopes, huh?"

"Maybe I intended to seduce you if you gave me a hard time."

"Damn it! In that case, I protest." He flung himself onto the mattress, crossed his legs at the ankle, showing off his sexy bare feet. Then he folded his hands behind his head, stretched out as if preparing to let her serve him.

The thought made her breathing quicken and her fingers ache to touch him. Especially along his rainbow tattoo, which decorated his side.

"Gav?" She kicked off her strappy sandals then climbed on the bed, kneeling beside him, wanting him to see how serious she was. "Time out a second, please?"

"Change your mind?" He sat up so he could look into her eyes, as if reassuring himself they were still on the same page.

"Not in the least. More like I want you to know how much I trust you. You were right earlier, when you said I liked it when you take control. Will you do more of that? Tie me up again?"

"Why?" He rubbed his chin. "Because *you* like it or because you're trying to prove some kind of point? Love, it was pretty apparent to me that—for whatever reason—you're still willing to give me free rein over your body when you let me fuck your tight ass last night."

"Mmm," she hummed.

"Yes, *mmm*, exactly," he echoed. "But seriously, Amber…"

Staring at her hands, which wrung each other in her lap, she said, "I guess I've just never had that before with a guy. I get off on it. I need more of that. I know things seem skewed one way right now, but there are things I want from you too. I trust you to help me loosen up. I don't want to always have to be the one who has everything in order. With you, I can live in the moment. You've taught me to do what I feel instead of relying on organization to keep everything in line."

"I can give you this," he promised. "It makes me feel like the man I used to be. Or better yet, the one I know I *can* still be, when I have you at my mercy. Because if someone as beautiful and strong as you has that much confidence in me, then how can I not believe in myself?"

"You should. So get to it." She poked his chest, hoping for the response she got.

Gavyn pounced, hauling her to the floor in a burst of motion even more impressive than she'd predicted. One she couldn't escape. He positioned her so she knelt with her ass on her heels and her palms on her thighs.

"Now that's a pretty sight," he crooned as he circled her, observing her from every angle. Intent on pleasing him, Amber sat up straighter. She put her shoulders back, thrusting out her breasts and looked up at him, waiting for further instructions.

"You were made for this, love." Gavyn cupped her face in his broad palm and she nuzzled into the sensual touch.

"I was made for *you*," she replied.

"No use in sweet-talking me now. You already gave yourself to me to play with." His thumbs tucked in his pockets and his fingers tapped against his jeans-clad legs as he considered what to do with her first.

Bending over, he snatched her scarf from the carpet and made his way behind her. When she instinctively turned, he took her shoulders in his hands and faced her forward again. Staying where he put her, she gasped when the silk of her scarf tickled the top of her arm, then along the edge of her bra before vanishing.

It returned on the sole of her foot, making her squeal and flinch, though she quickly restored her pose once she'd overcome her reflexive reaction.

"That's right, love," he purred. "You're going to be so good at this."

She might have asked what specifically he referred to if he hadn't chosen right then to loop the scarf around her face and blot out the light. Artificial darkness calmed her, making her focus on listening for Gavyn, as well as the raw feelings bombarding her.

"Your whole body relaxed just now," he said appreciatively. "Could you feel it?"

"Yes."

"That's how I want you to be, when we're together like this. You have nothing to worry about. Let me take care of you." A yelp escaped her when he unsnapped her bra. She hadn't been expecting his touch there.

He caressed her, stroking from her neck to the base of her spine and back before peeling the bra off her. The sound of it rustling to the floor seemed ten times louder to her as she relied on her other senses.

Her nipples puckered thanks to the air conditioning washing over her lightly perspiring skin.

Gavyn must have noticed because he reached over her, cupping her breasts, one in each palm. He squeezed them, then brushed his thumbs over the distended tips, making her squirm and lean forward, into his hold.

"You have amazing tits, Amber." He groaned, and she could imagine the jerk of his cock as he said it. "Maybe later, when I have you tied up, I'll fuck them. Would you like that?"

"Yes." It wasn't a lie. The thought of him using her body for his pleasure had her shivering in response.

"So would I." At some point, he must have circled her, coming to stand in front of her. He grasped the nape of her neck and pulled her face forward until she nuzzled the ultra-firm bulge in his pants.

The unique scent of him, soap and leather and man, had her ready to beg to taste him again. But she didn't have to. In the next moment, the sound of his zipper lowering rang in her ears. She licked her lips, arching her neck toward him.

"Open up, love." His request was followed by the blunt head of his cock, nudging her lips wider apart as he fed her his erection. It seemed even larger and heavier on her tongue when she couldn't see it.

Amber choked. He was quick to readjust, keeping her safe while ensuring they both derived maximum pleasure from the encounter. When she forgot everything except the soft moans he made as she suckled him and lifted her hands to his thighs, he growled, then pulled away.

"Put them down."

She obeyed instantly. Anything to get his cock inside her mouth again.

Only he didn't replace his shaft between her lips. "Better not let you get me too riled up. I want to take my time with you tonight."

If the nights he'd fucked her already were examples of him going quickly, she wasn't sure she could handle his idea of a marathon session. However, she wanted to try.

His hand fisted in her hair, tugging steadily until she followed his silent command, rising to her feet. When he kicked lightly at the insides of her ankles, she realized what he wanted and spread her legs wider.

"Good girl." He pressed his cheek to hers for a moment before slapping her ass, hard. "Stay there."

As if she had a choice unless she wanted to crash into the wall or something.

Still, it wasn't easy to remain immobile when she felt him kissing his way from her lips to her chin, down her neck, along her collarbones and lower. He paused to suckle first one nipple then the other, laving them until her knees wobbled, before proceeding to her belly.

When he arrived at her mound, he paused, breathing deep.

"I love how wet you get, Amber." He groaned as he slipped one finger beneath the elastic of her panties and into her as if he were checking her oil.

Her legs began to tremble, wishing he would fill her completely instead of teasing her with the tip of his finger.

"Eager?"

"Yes," she moaned.

"Then let me get these off of you." He surprised her again when he wrapped an arm around her, and lifted her, sweeping her underwear off with his other hand. His strength always impressed her. He underestimated himself, but she never would.

After setting her down and ensuring she was steady, he replaced his hand in her hair and used the leverage to lead her to the bed. When her knees knocked into the mattress, he gave her a tiny shove. She sprawled onto the plush duvet, bouncing a few times as she came to rest.

Gavyn surrounded one of her ankles with his hand and yanked, dragging it to the other side of the bed. She didn't mean to resist. What she really wanted was for him to climb on top of her and fuck. Hard and fast, until neither one of them could keep from exploding.

So when she tried to grab for him, she was surprised by his quick reactions. Or maybe he'd anticipated her move. He pinched her nipple, making her jerk and groan as the resulting sting turned to deep desire.

"Stay there."

She whimpered as his footsteps faded, though they didn't go far.

"I'm coming right back, love," he promised.

True to his word, something cool and satiny ran across her belly moments later. She gasped.

"Good thing we found another use for these ties." Chuckling deviously, he brushed one across her knee before wrapping it snugly around her ankle. "I don't plan on wearing them anymore once the business is up and running. At least they won't go to waste."

She expected him to take her bound leg and secure it to the bedpost. He did, though not to the one at the foot of the bed. No, he lifted her leg and tested the newfound flexibility she'd gained by practicing jivamukti with Sabra. He secured her feet to posts by her head, then got to work on her wrists. By the time Gavyn finished, he'd bound her with her legs spread and folded back, her hands held to her ankles, leaving her completely open and exposed to whatever he chose to do to her.

"Fuck me," she cried out when he blew a warm wash of his breath across her pussy.

"When I'm ready." He placed a series of kisses on her inner thigh, starting from her knee, working his way down. When he neared her core, he skipped across to the other side then repeated the torture there.

By the time his swirling tongue came in range of her clit, she was writhing, pleading shamelessly for his touch where she needed it most.

Gavyn hummed. "You're so beautiful when you beg."

This time he rewarded her not-so-patience. He feasted on her spread pussy, using his lips, tongue, and teeth. He pumped inside her, curling his fingers so that they pressed against the front wall of her pussy, bringing her to a fast orgasm.

In the darkness behind her blindfold, lights twinkled. There, with the ecstasy he gave her, she saw their rainbows swirling in front of her and nearly cried with relief and sheer delight.

Until he put his mouth over her again and began the process all over again.

Sensitive at first, she squirmed, unable to evade the lapping of his intentionally soft tongue. Before long, she didn't want to. Amber quit trying to regulate her pleasure. She allowed her body to respond to Gavyn in the way it was designed to.

She lost track of how many times he made her climax before he snapped.

With a curse, he lunged to the side, shaking the bed as he grabbed protection. Or at least she assumed he did. It blew her mind that she didn't even bother to ask him about that, wouldn't have even if she hadn't heard the crinkle of the package, confirming her suspicions, because she believed—all the way to her soul—that he would take care of her as he had sworn.

He verified that credence again when he filled her with his steely cock. His shaft felt twice as plump as she remembered, either from how he had her bound or because gifting her with so much bliss had turned him on.

In this position, he was able to play her mercilessly. His fingers wandered everywhere on her body, hitting the high points with regularity. When he pressed his thumb between her lips, she didn't have to be told to suck. Having him occupy almost every part of her drove her mad. Gavyn waited until she was delirious with passion before he pistoned into her while toying with her clit, ensuring she would come apart with a scream. How he managed to keep from pouring into her when she nearly strangled his thick shaft, she had no idea.

When she was panting, sweating and moaning his name on constant repeat, drowning in rapture, he finally leaned forward and removed the blindfold from her eyes.

She'd forgotten how bright it was, actually. Squinting, she peered up at Gavyn.

His face was flushed, making his stubble stand out in contrast. He had a feral light in his eyes that thrilled her and made her feel one hundred percent woman. Chest gleaming with sweat, and his muscles filled with blood, he took her breath away.

"I wanted you to see what you do to me, love," he practically snarled, at the edge of his super-human restraint. Leaning forward, he plowed into her while resting his hand on her throat. Enough to thrill her, though never enough to injure her or restrict her breathing. "I'm going to paint you with my come so you can see how fucking much I crave you. Of all things, I will never ration my lust for you. It won't be confined or limited. So I hope you like being fucked half to death every night. It's going to take about a thousand years before you don't have this impact on me anymore. Even then, I doubt I'll have enough of you."

The whole time he spoke to her, he plunged into her. It didn't take more than that before he had them both ready to shatter. How could she resist the candor of his passion?

The moment she quaked, her eyes fluttering as she fought to keep them open, to watch the man shuttling between her legs, he growled, "Come on me, now, before I have to pull out of this sweet pussy."

His dirty words and the desperation with which he roared them ensured she did as he said. The moment she had finished cresting, he withdrew, yanked off the condom then jerked himself so fast and hard that his hand blurred.

He shouted her name, then stayed true to his word. "Amber!"

Gavyn shot jet after jet of come on her breasts and belly. A few powerful spurts made it as far as her lips. She reached out her tongue to collect a stray droplet, causing another weaker pulse of pearly liquid to fall from his cock.

"You're mine, Amber." He spread the glistening fluid over her, massaging it into her skin.

"As long as you're mine too." She beamed as he untied her, tending to her carefully and

258

thoroughly, which was for the best since she didn't think she'd ever be able to move again.

"For as long as you'll have me, love."

Amber couldn't stop smiling even when she grew sleepy. Gavyn kept talking to her, low and sure as he picked her up, cradled her to his chest and carried her—floppy limbs and all—into the bathroom.

He climbed inside the tub and held her as he filled it with steamy water and plenty of bubbles, making sure to pamper her while washing the sticky mess he'd made off her skin. She was almost sad to see it go, having enjoyed being so definitively claimed as his.

Maybe he'd do it again soon.

Gavyn took excellent care of her. He cupped steaming water in his hands and poured it over her, delighting her super-sensitized skin with the trickles. Though he continued to thrill her, she loved simply reclining in his hold, soaking in the heat and strength of his muscled chest against her back. Exhausted, she still found it hard to relax completely following the chaos and excitement of the day. When all his pampering began to make arousal simmer low in her belly again, she couldn't believe it.

"The water's getting cold, love." He nuzzled the side of her face, delighting her with the rasp of his stubble. "Ready for bed?"

"With you? Always." She turned her head and kissed him one last time before he helped her stand long enough to dry her off with a plush towel. When she was set, he hastily did the same for himself.

Amber sighed as Gavyn carried her back to the bedroom, turned down the covers on the bed then slipped beneath them with her. Their legs tangled. They interlocked the rest of their bodies, her head resting on his chest while their arms wrapped around each other.

Even after another night overflowing with passion, she still found herself wanting more of him. What the hell had gotten into her?

When she shifted, restless, the steely length of his cock brushed her thigh. "You're hard again already?"

Thank God.

"Can't seem to help myself around you. Don't worry, love. It won't kill me." He misunderstood.

"More," she whispered, clearing up any confusion.

When he hesitated, she didn't. Amber reached over him to the stash of condoms on the nightstand and ripped one open with her teeth. Then she slid her hand between them and covered him, making them both moan when his cock jumped at her touch.

This time she curled onto her side, with Gavyn behind her, spooning her. He took the invitation and fit himself to her from the rear. It took several pumps of his hips to embed himself fully with her legs pressed together and her pussy swollen from the fucking he'd already given her.

Once they were connected again, he took his time, pressing up into her then pulling away, putting a sliver of space between them before returning. It was leisurely and more for the low level arousal that lingered while they made love than for the payoff of a brilliant orgasm. His hand wandered down her front to her mound where he rubbed gently. When she couldn't stand to watch anymore or end their ride too soon, she turned her head to the side and claimed his mouth.

They kissed slowly, and deeply, just like their souls merged.

It went on forever, until they pushed their luck a bit too far and one perfectly placed flick of his finger over her clit sent her into a deceptively strong climax.

The milking of her pussy lured Gavyn into joining her. He cried out her name as he came, locked deep within her.

"Gavyn," she replied. "I love you."

If possible, he came harder, grunting as he spilled the last of his seed. He clutched her tightly as he gave her every bit of him that she'd earned. And when he'd regained the ability to speak, he looked into her eyes and vowed, "I love you too."

"Does this mean we finally get to sleep together, Gav?" she asked lazily, her eyes already halfway shut.

"Mmm hmm. Tonight and every night if I have my say," he swore to her.

"Sounds like a plan to me."

"You and your plans." Gavyn chuckled as he snuggled her close then rambled, as if already drifting off. "Just out of curiosity, what happens when a wedding planner gets married?"

"I guess we'll have to find out someday." She smiled, hoping it might storm so they could enjoy the rainbows together.

And in the morning, he was right where he'd promised. Closer, really, since he woke her with another helping of phenomenal sex.

That would never get old.

EPILOGUE

Tom London sat on a stool at the bar in the Hot Rods' kitchen. His boot heels hooked onto the bottom rung. With his knees splayed, he leaned on his forearms, which were braced on his thighs. Willie was beside him and he couldn't help but reach over to hold her hand. It felt right, since their combined families spread out around them, completely integrated. Nola and Kaige cuddled together on the couch with Ambrose sleeping peacefully in her daddy's arms. Quinn was on the floor playing video games with Roman and Alanso, while Buster lay nearby, resting his head on the boy's thigh.

Amber and Kaelyn were brainstorming details for some upcoming event on their plate while Gavyn stared dreamily at the woman he was madly in love with. Eli, Sally, Bryce, Holden, Sabra—who held Fuzzi—and Carver were videochatting with the Powertools crew.

From where he sat, Tom could see the image of his nephew, Joe, who lounged with his wife Morgan in his lap and his own kid playing nearby. Abby and Nathan, always together, made him chuckle. Tom hoped Ambrose would have some more brothers, sisters or cousins of her own to have fun with soon.

All of them had had their ups and downs, but they were here, surviving...no, *thriving* despite the bad times they'd overcome.

Good food and better company made the fairly average Sunday feel like the biggest of celebrations to Tom.

It would only be better if Willie was officially his instead of dodging him again in whatever crazy game she'd been playing with his heart.

"We've done pretty damn fine job, I'd say." She smiled over him as he surveyed their domain and the family they'd raised.

"Not too shabby," he agreed. "Now that they're taken care of, I think it's time to focus on other projects."

"What?" She looked away, though she knew damn well what he meant.

"It's been a long time coming," Tom said as he nodded at her. "Now that all of them are on the right road, I think I should pay some attention to myself. You too, for that matter."

"Tommy, I don't think—"

He refused to let her run anymore. "Look, I understand that the past wasn't kind to either of us in the love department. But if our kids are brave enough to take those chances, then I can be too."

Willie shook her head vehemently. "They're betting in a game with stakes they don't understand. We did too when we were young and foolish. I've already been broken, and I don't have any reserves to play with these days."

"Maybe I'm getting dumber as I get older, but I'm ready to be stupid again." He leaned forward then. "Get ready, Willie, I'm coming for you. I've been told that I can be kind of a stubborn ass when there's something I want."

"Now *that* I don't doubt." She drew her fingers from his and crossed her arms over her ample breasts. Unfortunately for her, being pissed off only made her look more fierce and that was one of the things he loved most about her.

Tom laughed so loud, everyone turned to stare at his riotous outburst.

Let them look.

They might all be a bit surprised soon, when they saw what he had in store for one delectable and fiery Ms. Wilhelmina Brown.

He might be past his prime, but he wasn't dead yet.

THE ADVENTURES DON'T END HERE! KEEP READING...

The best things are worth waiting for.

Tom London has done a pretty damn good job. Despite an illness that stole his young wife years ago, he's raised his biological son, and several adopted ones, to be fine men. The Hot Rods might be unconventional, but they're hardworking, hard-playing, and hard-loving. Tom couldn't ask for anything more—except perhaps an equally fierce love of his own. And he's got his eye on a luscious candidate. Ms. Wilhelmina Brown, a longtime widow with more than enough sass in her step to take him on.

Willie has a lot in common with Tom. She's raised two wonderful daughters, both now married into the Hot Rods family, and lived through her own tragedy, having lost her husband in a horrific accident. More than two decades later, she and Tom still live with the ghosts of their pasts, but she'd have to be dead herself not to feel the man's effect on her libido. They already share a mutual respect; perhaps they can each be what the other needs in more tangible ways...

As Tom and Willie take one step closer, an explosive revelation shoots them several steps back. But that bombshell turns out to be just a precursor to something potentially worse...potentially deadly...and potentially enough to keep the mature lovers apart forever.

EXCERPT FROM LONG TIME COMING, HOT RODS BOOK 8

Wilhelmina Brown couldn't believe she'd been married for seven full years. People had said she and Steven would never last when they'd tied the knot the day after high school graduation. She was happy to prove them wrong. Looking at the two precious children they'd made, who slept together on a pullout couch in the tiny yet spotless living room, she couldn't have been prouder or more content.

Hopefully, her husband would enjoy the dinner she'd cooked to celebrate their milestone and the time they'd had together. The roast was the prime cut of the latest slaughter from the Berry Family Farm down the road from the house they shared on the outskirts of town. She'd bartered some extra sewing to supplement her grocery money for the splurge. Rural Mississippi life had to have some perks. After all, inclusion certainly wasn't one of them.

She tried not to think of some people's outdated ignorance and the hatred they tried to inject into her relationship with Steven, simply because her skin was drastically darker than his. Or how he'd been passed over for promotions after he'd brought her to the company picnic. Or her guilt about the way even some lifelong friends had treated him, turned on him, since he dared to love her.

Not tonight.

Sometimes it felt as if it was them against the world. She was okay with that. With a partner like him at her back, she could manage pretty much anything.

Willie tidied the already neat kitchen then fussed with her hair and the skirt of the pink dress she'd made while she waited for her husband, who frequently doubled up on his shifts for overtime. Maybe they'd get lucky and the girls would sleep straight through the night. They were almost always in bed by the time their daddy got home. In the cramped quarters, they often woke up to sneak in a visit before Willie and Steven were ready to go to sleep in the house's single bedroom. She probably shouldn't let them stay up so late so often, but when she saw how happy the playtime made her children and her husband alike, she didn't have the heart to put her foot down.

Willie checked the clock on the wall.

Wouldn't it figure that Steven was running even later than usual?

She peeked in at the supper, breathed deep, drew the savory aroma into her lungs, then crumpled the tinfoil over the baking pan tighter to keep the meat warm without drying it out.

***

An hour later, it was pretty clear something had gone horribly wrong.

Willie sat with the phone on the kitchen table in front of her, twisting the spiral cord in her fingers as she waited for Steven to call and explain whatever fluke had kept him at the factory where he welded hot water heater tanks, or how he'd run out of gas, or...something.

He never did.

Instead, a loud triple knock on the front door had her shooting out of the kitchen chair so fast it toppled to the outdated harvest-gold linoleum behind her. The kids woke at the crash. Nola began to cry when Willie darted past her and her older sister—Amber, who comforted her sibling—to answer the door.

"Shush, it's okay," she lied to them as she paused, her fingers wrapped around the knob, afraid to turn it and change her life forever.

Alternating red and blue washes of light painted her babies' lovely mocha skin ghastly unnatural shades.

Right then, she knew she'd relive this moment in her nightmares for the rest of her life.

The pounding on the door came again, startling her into action.

Before she could stop herself, she opened it—just a little, like Steven had shown her. She peeked from inside the safe haven they'd built together at the police officers standing on her cracked front stoop.

"Mrs. Brown?" the taller of the two asked with a grimace.

"Yes." Her heart pounded so fast and so hard that she had trouble hearing her own voice. Or maybe it was merely a wisp compared to usual.

"I regret to inform you that there's been an accident." He paused and swallowed. "A bad one. It's your husband, ma'am."

"No!" As if it would block out the terrible news she'd never be able to unhear, she lifted the hem of her apron, covering her face with the gingham material Steven had salvaged from a stained tablecloth at the Salvation Army for her last birthday.

It seemed as if her children understood the cops when their wails escalated to shrieks. Or maybe that was her making those strangled sobs.

"He's hurt?" She tried to keep herself together in case she could go to him, help him to fight.

The stockier officer came to his partner's aid. "There was no chance for survival. The car was completely destroyed in the collision with a delivery truck. Then it spun off the road, crashed through the railing on Jefferson's Bridge and went into the river. With all the rain we've had lately, he washed away before anyone could even think of assisting. I'm very sorry."

Willie's knees buckled. She fell to the ground, gasping for air through the searing pain in her chest, which resulted from her shattering heart. Was this what Steven had felt like in those final moments?

If it weren't for the girls behind her, she would have let herself wither away and rejoin her husband. Amber and Nola screamed a chorus of "Momma, Momma!" endlessly, as if they could tell how desperately Willie needed a reason to pick herself up.

Somehow she would do it.

She had to.

For them, the only remaining pieces of her husband in the world.

ABOUT THE AUTHOR

Jayne Rylon is a *New York Times* and *USA Today* bestselling author. She received the 2011 RomanticTimes Reviewers' Choice Award for Best Indie Erotic Romance.

Her stories used to begin as daydreams in seemingly endless business meetings, but now she is a full-time author, who employs the skills she learned from her straight-laced corporate existence in the business of writing. She lives in Ohio with two cats and her husband, the infamous Mr. Rylon.

When she can escape her purple office, Jayne loves to travel the world, SCUBA dive, take pictures, avoid speeding tickets in her beloved Sky and—of course—read.